MW00825345

Cat-A-Tonic Book 01:

Marcus' Misadventures

By Jeremy M. Moore

Copyright © 2021 Jeremy M. Moore

All Rights Reserved

Dedications:

To all the pets I've had over the years, who shared their unconditional love with me and my family. You will always bring joy into our days, even if it also means a little chaos.

To my wife, Kim, who inspires me to change the world and see the magic in everything.

Table of Contents

Prologue

A man, woman, and large white cat sat side by side on metal folding chairs. While free to move from their seats, none were in any position to leave the area. Large flood lamps shone into their faces, preventing them from seeing the shadowy figures behind the lights. The figures moved about, murmuring among themselves. What was being said was impossible for the trio to make out, but *how* it was being said was not reassuring.

The man was dressed in a long coat, jeans, and a torn-up t-shirt bearing an obscure cartoon. He was covered head to toe in various bandages and wraps, giving him the appearance of a half-finished mummy. His only serious injury seemed to be a splint on his arm. His curiosity seemed to have gotten the better of him as he attempted to make out the shadowy persons behind the lights. When he found he could not identify any distinguishing features, his attention shifted to the room, then to the lights themselves. Each time he tried to speak, a cough from the woman caused him to remain silent.

Beside him, a woman in pink workout attire sat with a glum look on her face. Her brow creased while she waited. She looked inconvenienced as she studied the ground, angry and disinterested in the delay, but every so often, her ear would twitch, or her eyes would shift to the shadows. For now, she was content to gauge the tone and nature of the hushed conversations. If she could just make out what was being said, she might have a better opportunity to prepare her answers.

The third seated occupant, a large, fluffy white cat, sat annoyed at the very existence of this tribunal. From what he could gather, this was merely human meowing and pointless chatter, and he had to attend to important activities at home. Namely, he needed to nap upon his tower and have the fanciest of feasts brought to him by his human servants. Instead of doing any of these things, he now sat on a chair like some trained fool. It was almost to the level of being a dog, and that offended him to his core. The simpletons beside him sat obediently in their chairs, but he expected humans to abide by such silly rules. As a cat, he would partake in this game of words only until it fully bored him. At the very least, the annoying beings that wanted him to sit on this chair had taken care of his wounds and provided him a nice plush pillow on which to sit while they wasted his time. He considered not biting them when this was over, but that would depend on how much of his time they wasted with their questions.

A mechanical click came from behind the lights, and a deep voice spoke. A device altered the figure's voice, protecting the speaker's identity. All the shadows spoke in the same monotone, echoing voice.

"Please state your names for the record," the mystery voice announced, followed by a pop as the microphone cut back off.

"Marcus Kyle," the man replied.

"Just your name," the shadowy figure added. "We do not need your title, Magus. To clarify, your name is Kyle…"

Marcus let out a long, soulful sigh. There was an old agitation and weariness to the sound. In the past, he might have laughed at the mix-up or mispronunciation, but after hearing it so many times over the past few days, he found the joke had worn out its welcome. "You know, that was funny at first, but—"

"Just your name," the voice repeated.

"My name," he said, putting emphasis on his words, "is Marcus—with a C, not a G—Kyle."

The figures debated for a moment, muttering among themselves before one approached the microphone and spoke. "Isn't Kyle a first name?"

If the first sigh had been long, this one was an eternity that bordered on a breakdown. "Yes, but it's an old name. It comes from—"

"Ah," the figure replied in a disinterested tone. "Your name, miss?"

"Alana Kym," she answered, folding her arms over her chest. "And yes, my surname can also be a first name. Do you want me to spell it? It's K-Y-M."

A loud scratch of pen on paper came over the speaker, as something on the figure's notes were crossed out. "No need, Ms. Kym," the voice replied in a flat tone. Alana's face soured.

Another pause followed, and a series of scribbling noises came over the crackle of the microphone. "Oh... oh my, yes, that is quite enough, Mr. Purloin. Again, please accept our apologies for— Yes, we understand the insult." There was a fear, and a bit of reverence, in the voices now.

"Are you talking to my cat?" Marcus looked between the

darkened shapes and the annoyed cat on the pillow. "You can speak feline? Why does Savannah's police force have a cat whisperer?"

"We are asking the questions here, Mr. Magus," they stated. "What we can and cannot do is not up for discussion now. But in the interest of cooperation between civilians and law enforcement... Yes."

Marcus' eyebrow rose and he tried to fold his arms only for a sharp pain to remind him of his injury.

"Now, why don't you all tell us how... this"—there was the general disturbance of a shadowy arm waving toward the three of them— "all happened?"

Marcus, Purloin, and Alana looked at each other. The cat huffed, laying his head on the pillow as Alana shook hers. "Fine, you can start. Just try to be brief... this time."

His apprehension from moments ago forgotten, Marcus Kyle smiled from ear to ear and turned a little too quickly to his inquisitors. "This will sound strange, but it all started one sunny day when..."

Chapter 1: Little Red Book

One day I'm going to be somebody.

At least that was what I'd told myself every day since I was little. I'd always wanted to accomplish something amazing. I would get all the glory and praise that came with it. Changing the world with my brilliance and know-how.

So, when I tell you I was a file clerk in a document storage room, you probably can see how well that was all going. I spent most of my time interacting more with stacks of papers and binders than with people. Since it was a secure room built back in the ages when people said "aught" for the year, it was like being locked in a prison from the Middle Ages. Things got dropped off to be filed away and it was my job to update a database with the location code numbers, contents, and so many other boring things you've probably already stopped listening to me at this point.

You would think, *But, Marcus, isn't your job at a super-successful pharmaceutical company? Surely, you must see all kinds of cool stuff, right?*

First, I'll spare you the obvious "Shirley" joke, because I'm a man of culture who does not settle for low-hanging puns. I find them *pun-gent.* Next, you'd be wrong. What I saw was just data and spreadsheets, maybe the occasional CD or those big black scientific journals. The only good part about my job, besides the fact that it allowed me to pay bills, was people left me alone to do my thing. The work was simple, and after years of doing it, I could file a day's worth of material in a matter of minutes, which left me alone in the quiet depths. So, I'd often catch up on my emails, read books on my tablet, and consider what would lead to my big break toward fame.

Sometimes I'd venture into the far reaches of the vault, down hallways that were carved into ancient bedrock long before they were coated in modern concrete. It was a forgotten world down here, and I was the King of Lost Things. I'd made it my mission to quest into the furthest depths to see exactly what was back there. A few times I encountered ancient technology, such as a beta-max tape, and when I discovered microfiche had nothing to do with sea life, it was devastating and made all those old spy movies a lot less funny.

Still, I enjoyed opening old boxes and verifying their contents against the database. You know, to keep the boxes honest. When I could muster up the will to delve into our backlog, I always learned something new. Nothing I read helped me get ahead in the company, but it painted a mental picture of life at Wonderland Pharmaceuticals over the decades. Honestly, I wished I thought to do it more often, but since no one ever asked about stuff from well over fifty years ago, I never made it a priority. Going through them was like stepping into a forgotten age where people wore funny hats, had obnoxious-sized beards, and smoked while working in the labs.

Today was a special day. I'd received a request for some of the oldest boxes we had on file. So, with my trusty two-wheel cart, which I named "Cartly," we ventured into the furthest reaches of the vault.

My remark about the archive being a prison wasn't just a snappy observation or a witty comment on how working in an office could feel. No, I meant it literally. The facility was a pre-Civil War prison here in Savannah, Georgia. I don't know how long it worked in that capacity, because details from that time are sketchy. This was all long before Vincent Payne, founder and CEO of Wonderland Pharmaceuticals, came along. Technically, it was his grandfather, or great-grandfather, who started the "Dynasty of Wonder" that was our company. In the end, it was a Payne that turned a historical eyesore and a dangerously dilapidated structure into one of the biggest employers in Savannah.

Everything above ground was new, innovative, and growing. Down here in the forgotten roots, history stayed neatly buried with me as its only companion. When the renovation teams had emptied the holding cells of their contents, some parts were so ingrained that they could never be removed. One example: the large metal plates on the wall that had been used to anchor chains. Another would be the occasional series of parallel holes on the floor where prison bars had once been. They filled the round holes with newer concrete, but if you spent as much time here as me, you could see the subtle difference in color, even after all these years. Plus, they were not smooth to roll over, and more than once Cartly tipped, causing boxes to spill everywhere. Looking at these echoes of the past had me pulling my fleece a little closer. My chill wasn't just from the temperature.

We ventured further back into the archive than I had ever gone before, back to a spot where the shelves were lined with dust. Back here, it had that old-book smell, like an ancient library.

Averting my eyes, I tried not to think about the nature of the experimental records we had back here. Modern research reports were lines of data that had been run through simulations and test modules. But these old records… well there was always a hint of malice behind the method, like just getting the answer wasn't enough. The few reports I had skimmed over the years recorded things like emotional and physical reaction by test subjects. Most of the *volunteers* were animals… most. Humanity hasn't always had the kindest eyes when looking at their fellow man, especially those that were incarcerated. Thinking about the kinds of things in this forgotten archive, and the dark history it catalogued, could make a lesser person get lost in their thoughts and go mad from the revelations.

"Thank goodness I have you with me to stay sane, right, Cartly?" Checking the paperwork, I started piling up the boxes until a cloud of dust caused me to cough and wheeze until I was leaning on Cartly for support. "I wish I had your constitution. You're never bothered by the dust. Guess you are made of tougher stuff." All my attempt at humor earned me was more coughing, but I still thought it was worthwhile.

With tears in my eyes and my throat refusing to let me breathe normally, I cursed myself for not bringing a bottle of water.

These back areas could be hard on a person's lungs. Since breathing

was an activity I enjoyed, I sped up on my way back to my desk to

get a drink. As I came up one slope, one of Cartly's wheels caught

on the uneven flooring and jostled the boxes. I shifted my arms,

trying to correct and adjust before everything spilled out. With so

many years of experience and my mad carting skills, I moved with

the bump and kept everything vertical. I had learned to expect the

treacherous floor, but on that day a fresh problem occurred. There

was a sudden hiss before the cart bucked hard to one side, sending

boxes toppling to the floor. Examining Cartly's wheel, I found a

large packaging staple jutting out. "Damn, and he was only two

weeks to retirement."

Scooping up files and journals before dropping them back

into the closest container, I kept coughing. The old boxes were thick

with dust, which I inhaled as I kneeled among scattered papers,

journals, and folders. Reaching behind me, there was a jolt of pain

on my fingertips, causing me to pull away. Looking for the source of

my pain, I expected to find I had touched a shelf or something metal

from inside a box. I was a little afraid I might have grazed a socket

and narrowly avoided electrocuting myself. If that had been the case, there was no telling how many hours might pass before someone found me. The thought of dying from something so stupid in a small place like this sent a chill down my spine. Instead, to my confused relief, all I found behind me was a single red booklet. Unlike the piles of journals and notes, it was pocket-sized, and I stuffed it into my fleece to get it off the floor while I continued cleaning.

Something glittered on the ground where the book had been, a small empty vial. I picked it up with a grimace, unsure what had been inside this old vial and why it was being stored instead of tossed out. I was about to throw the old glass into my desk's bin when the fluorescent lights reflected off the crystalized contents and glittered in a rainbow of colors. Inserting a pen into the empty tube, I moved it over to my desk for further examination. Unsure of what was inside, I decided it was best not to touch old chemicals. After all, I had already been shocked once by something in that box. There was no need to risk getting contaminated with ancient unknown experiments, but I also couldn't just throw out something so cool looking. For now, it could brighten up my desk for a few hours, before I made a trip to the labs to properly dispose of it.

After carrying each individual box up to the front counter, I plopped the vial-covered pen into an old coffee cup filled with all the other oddball items I'd found over the years. Then I rattled off an email asking to have someone come pick up the boxes. Out of the corner of my eye, I saw a blinking light on my phone showing several missed messages. All of them were from the same person and had come in over the last few minutes.

"Of all the days to lose track of time," I muttered as I gathered up my things and sprinted to the parking lot.

Chapter 2: Lunch with Alana

As I exited the building at a mad dash, a sharp honking of a car horn caught my attention, and I headed in its direction. Giving a quick wave to the driver, I trotted over to open the passenger door. "Hey, Alana. Sorry to keep you waiting. I was in the back forty and had to pull some old boxes. When I saw all your messages I realized how late it had gotten."

"Seat belt," my fiancée barked, checking the mirrors and preparing to move. "You know we don't have a lot of time for lunch, especially if you're always running late. There will be just enough time to get there and back, and that is without dillydallying." She gave me an obviously irritated look, since I was not already in the car and buckled up. "Today, Marcus."

Fastening my seatbelt and only partially pinching myself with the quick motion, I gave her a thumbs-up. "Sorry, Alana," I repeated. "You know I get poor reception in my prison cell."

"Former prison," she corrected before pulling out into traffic. "You know the company hates people talking about the building's history."

"Right." I nodded, feeling a pain in my side. Something in

my pocket had a sharp corner. Wincing, I adjusted and tried to change the topic. Alana was still in her dour work mode, very clinical and correcting, and that would make for a long lunch. "Still, it's great that we can both take time away to go out for lunch, right? It's been a long time since we had the chance."

"Yeah. It has." Checking the rearview mirror, she shook her head. "Maybe we should go back. I can get something in the cafeteria. We can go out to dinner this weekend instead of rushing for lunch. I've got so much to do at work, and—"

"And this is what a fiancé is for: to prevent burnout by getting you to step away for a few minutes. Isn't that right, Ms. Kym?"

Alana growled, debating if my use of her last name was worse than my being right. She hated leaving in the middle of anything, especially now that her project on genetic modifications was in the last stages. Her creased brow and narrow glare told me she was still processing some detail or result.

On a normal day, Alana would be eager to leave the office and stretch her legs. While she loved her job, as it let her pursue her passions, she also enjoyed a break to clear her mind. If she was grumpy, it meant something wasn't going according to plan. "Rough day? I'm sure things will look better after lunch."

Alana shrugged at my comment. My words didn't seem very effective, which made sense. She had a Master's degrees in Genetics and Chemistry, and had an intimate knowledge of every aspect of her project. All I knew how to do was mix chemicals and see what happened. It's not that I didn't want to learn, but there was so much to know that I felt overwhelmed. I could file a report like it was nobody's business, but for lab work I would Ibe starting from scratch.

From what I understood of the lab work our company conducted, it was mostly watching boring looking chemicals mix and boil for several hours. There weren't any bubbling test tubes or crazy coiled tubes, and they didn't even wear white lab coats. In fact, I recently learned most chemicals were off-white, so it wasn't even like they got to watch colors change. When I was a kid, I had a toy car that at least changed color under hot and cold water.

Alana assured me this new project was groundbreaking and exciting work in genome manipulation and the harvesting of residual dormant DNA. From what I understood it meant Wonderland

Pharmaceuticals was trying to bring back old traits people used to have, like being naturally stronger or maybe more resistant to environmental conditions? I'm sure there is more to it than that, but my brain just does not seem wired for science.

The point was this project was her pride and joy, and the CEO himself had been demanding daily updates. Alana would always tell me about the revolutionary nature of her work, and that it was a game changer in the world of genetic research.

"I suppose," Alana muttered, taking a hard right into the restaurant parking lot. While I would never call her an unsafe driver, she had a blunt style. Fond of hard turns and braking, she drove with skills but lacked the smooth finesse that would have made it a comfortable ride. We always arrived safely, if sore and a little battered. I often offered to drive, but she refused, saying it calmed her and she liked the control of being behind the wheel. The creases on the steering wheel seemed to contradict her claims.

Exiting the car, we were greeted by a refreshing cool breeze. It was early spring, that time of year when it was warm enough to sit outside but summer's blazing heat hadn't yet set in. The winds were refreshing, not hot and muggy. Large willow trees stretched their limbs to form a canopy over an outdoor patio, providing shade and the feeling of eating in a pocket tucked away from the hustle and bustle of the modern world.

As we settled into our table, another pain shot up my side. Pulling the offending object from my fleece pocket, Alana looked at me with concern. "Please tell me you haven't been reading books at work again."

"Okay, I won't tell you that." I laughed, examining the cover. "This fell out of a box at work. I put it in my pocket as I was cleaning, just to get it off the floor. That happened right before I came to meet you. I must have forgotten it was there." Turning it over in my hands, I snorted and read the title aloud. Embroidered with the simple golden line art of a lion's head mid-roar, the cover's title rested between its teeth and read *C.A.T.: Tricks and Tips*.

Alana rolled her eyes, then returned to her menu. "C.A.T.: Tricks and Tips? That doesn't sound like anything related to work at all. Probably from someone's desk from way back when. I bet they just wanted to have it destroyed to make room for newer documents."

While I agreed on some level, there was something off about this book. Like when I would find a rare collectors' copy or collectible. I didn't want to see something so old, and possibly precious, get destroyed just to make room on a shelf. "Do you think they'd let me keep it?"

"Why would you need another cat book? Don't you have enough? There are stacks of books all over the house that you 'had to have' and have not even cracked open yet. Besides, you will never get Purloin to listen to you long enough to learn any tricks."

Just to be contentious, I opened the book and started reading the prologue aloud. "Welcome to the world of magic, future magus." Grinning, I turned to her. "That is almost my name. Magus, Marcus. Sounds like fate to me."

With a teacher's patience, she shook her head. "A magus is a sorcerer, a learned person of distinction. You're a wise guy on your best day."

"You hold in your hand the book of C.A.T. tips and tricks for beginners. This is book one in a series that will lead you down a road of wonderment and magic. I hope the mystic knowledge within these pages will be a boon to you and yours and not a burden as so many have found it to be in the past. The contents *do* contain what you seek, but if I may impart some hard-learned wisdom of my own, it will not be in the manner you are accustomed. You may find by the end of this book you have undertaken more than you intended, but once something is learned, it cannot be forgotten easily. Retrieving hidden-away secrets like this can change the world and will certainly change you. Whether that be for the best or worst will be at your discretion."

"If, when you finish your time with this book, you still seek additional knowledge, I encourage you to seek out the rest of our series. Sincerely yours, Alister." Closing the book, anxiety twinged across my heart. "That was a lot of mumbo jumbo talk for something about cats. You don't see books like this anymore."

Alana nodded but otherwise remained focused on her menu and analyzing the options within. She was much more health-conscious than me and probably had been considering lunch options the entire day so she could find the most nutritional and balanced meal. I was not programmed to eat smart. Instead, I went for what looked best on the menu.

People always commented on how we were so different. She was athletic, health-conscious, practical, thoughtful, and tough. In fact, her being so strong was how our relationship began. I was taking out my trash one night when I rounded the corner and startled her. She must have thought I was a threat and responded with a quick jab to my face. When I got up, I remembered thinking about the cuteness of the woman hovering over me. I also remembered wondering why my face hurt so much. In the end, you could say I was love-*struck*. After that, we started talking. One thing led to another, and we got engaged. I wish I could say the courtship was an adventure, but really, it was just the same story of two people meeting by chance and liking each other.

People said I was "lucky to have her." I guess that would be the polite way of saying I wasn't a bad person, but nothing special. While Alana might be happy with our current way of life, I'd always hoped and waited for that big thing, for something fantastic to happen. Then maybe they would all stop seeing me as a shadow on stage. I liked to think I was a simple man. I'd settle for some simple quest or mission, like an alien princess falling from the sky, with Alana and I being her only hope, ancient jewelry needing to be melted down, or sparkly wish-granting gems begging to be discovered.

But in the end, my life had always just seemed mundane. Filing paperwork, arguing with an inanimate cart, and reading about people doing things while I sat locked away in my concrete tomb.

There had to be more to life than the simple nine-to-five, an adventure that didn't involve powering on my Mobile Gamestation X and waiting for updates. People told me all the fantasy novels I read had warped my head and the stacks of books all over our townhouse might just prove them right. In my defense, I was always trying new things, experimenting in my own way. An entire room of our home was filled with my previous attempts at grandeur, a museum with artifacts of failed glories: poorly sewn costumes, various pickled fruits and vegetables, homeopathic kits, and a miniature library of books on robotics, gemstones, mythologies, and symbols throughout history. The problem was that none of them ever captured my attention for long, but I kept looking. I was sure one day something would click.

Turning away from my darker thoughts, I flipped the book in my hands. Years in an archive and being a collector of books gave me some knowledge on assessing them. My first impression was that it was old. Not just in terms of being written a long time ago, but the style of the cover art, the title, and the type of language set it further back. While I might have thought of it as a gag gift, now I was wondering if this might be an antique or maybe a personal journal. If so, that was even more reason to prevent it from being destroyed. Inside, there were simple illustrations, diagrams, and walls of text. It was like a handwritten school textbook. Some words were faded, while others hard to make out, since the ink was smudged. More than likely, this was caused by the writer turning pages before it had time to dry. The thought brought a smile to my face. It was part of the charm of old books; looking through them was like peering through time or into another world.

"Weird," I muttered while trying to focus on the pages. "I've skimmed through a few chapters, and it seems like all it has is chemistry theorics, drawings, and recipes."

"You found a chemistry book in the archive of a pharmaceutical company, and you think that's weird?" Alana answered, mulling over each side of the menu for at least the fifth time since I sat down. "Please put the book away. I ordered some appetizers while you've been distracted with that book, and we are on the clock. Why don't you go wash up before the food gets here? You have no idea where that book has been."

"Yeah, I do it's been on a dusty shelf in a former prison cell for the last bajillion years." A quick glance from Alana stopped me from saying anything more. Before admitting defeat, I flipped to the last page. There I found a single paragraph written in an intricately detailed cursive font and laughed. "You may wonder why a book with a title about cat tricks has had no instructions for tricks for cats included. That is the trick. Cats do not need instructions. Only those of us on two legs need orders. Still, I hope this book has been enlightening for you and that you learned all the secrets it holds. Alister (again)." I closed the book with a loud clap, set it down, and took a picture of the cover with my phone.

This piqued my curiosity. There was no way I would not do a deeper dive into the origin of this book. What did "C.A.T." mean? Based on the cover and title, the author clearly had some interest in felines, but everything I had skimmed over was about chemistry and theorems. If this was a scientific journal, why go all out on a detailed, eye-catching cover? If this was someone's journal, why hadn't a relative claimed it by now?

The more I focused on this book, the more my mind whirled in search of an answer. It was an itch at the back of my brain that I could not scratch. Sure, I had that reaction to a lot of series, but this held an air of urgency, like getting a letter from the government around tax time. I needed to read more. After all, what was the worst that could happen? I guessed I might waste time looking up an old book and get another reprimand for doing research during working hours. Being punished for research at a research manufacturing lab would be some dark humor, I supposed, but it wasn't like I'd lose my job over it. No one really wanted to do my job, and I'd heard the office chatter. Office chairs got more consideration and praise than I ever would by working in the chamber of lost paperwork.

Looking up from my phone, I saw that Alana's face had turned pink. Out of the corner of my eye, I could see a few confused glances being cast our way by people passing by. Unlike me, she did not seek the spotlight. Unfortunately, my desire for any excitement and for anything to happen often meant it caught her in my call-to-attention radius. One day, I knew, it would all pay off and I would stop being on the sidelines and the center spotlight would be on me.

She could focus on her projects while I grew in the sun. Before she could say anything, our appetizers arrived. Alana gave a quick thank-you to the server as she placed her napkin on her lap. She took a moment to compose herself. "You wanted to read a book of tricks. It sounds like the only trick is that it's about chemistry."

"Maybe, but I think there is something to this thing. I'll do some research and see what I can find out. It's probably nothing exciting, just an old textbook, and the publisher wanted to have a cool cover to sell more copies. I just hope this doesn't lead to me being bamboozled by some old-timey flimflam man, especially one who wrote a book that no one has read in ages."

"Maybe you should start by updating your vocabulary to the twenty-first century. 'Flimflam man,' 'bamboozled.' Seriously, who talks like that anymore?" While she meant the words as a barb, her lips curled at the corners. Her playful personality was peeking through her gloomy mood. The world might laugh at me, but I could always count on Alana to laugh *with* me.

"All that chemistry stuff, it might be something you'd like." I reached out for one appetizer, only to pull my hand back when Alana's napkin snapped out like a cloth whip. "Hey!"

"Marcus," she warned, recoiling for another strike. "We've been over this. Wash your hands after touching old books. You don't want to contaminate our food, do you?"

"I'm sure it's fine, Alana. Live a little." I cast her my best disarming smile, but she was as immovable as a brick wall.

"Says the man who has ordered the same food here *every* time we come." She nodded towards the restaurant door. "Go wash your hands, please. Then we can eat."

"I don't order the *same* thing every time," I offered with a dismissive shake of my finger. "Sometimes they get better pictures of other burgers." Once she rolled her eyes, I rose from my chair and went to wash up.

As I left, Alana took the appetizer I had almost touched. Was she concerned about me washing my hands or did she just want that one in particular?

I will spare you the details of my bathroom adventures but will let you know it was as exciting and riveting as you imagine. On my way back to the table, I paused at the patio door, checking to make sure no one was right behind me so I could stand still for a moment. Call me an old romantic, or a cheesy goofball, but sometimes I just liked to stare like a schoolboy at my fiancée, to see her when she didn't know I was looking. I don't mean that in a creepy way, just that sometimes people put on faces when they know they're being watched and you get to see another side of them when they aren't wearing their social mask.

Alana sat in the sun, leaving the shady spot for me, her red hair churning in the light like molten lava. She looked toward the front door, probably guessing that was the path from where I would exit and not suspecting my crafty plan of coming out a side door. She took another bite of our appetizer. As she chewed, she looked at the book. Maybe it was the way the light reflected off the golden cover font or the odd designs, but she considered it with a healthy amount of curiosity. I wondered if we both could sense that there was something off about this book, a force that compelled her to reach out and seize it.

Her hand moved toward it; fingers outstretched. Just when I thought she would grab it, she pulled back in confusion. She bit her lip, her head tilting slightly as she considered something. Then, with a shrug, she dismissed the thought and reached out again for the book. Almost immediately, she pulled back with a yelp, throwing a napkin over the red book as if it were a violent insect.

Hearing her shriek, I broke off my stakeout and sprinted to the table. "What happened?"

"The book shocked me," she said, checking for injuries. "That really hurt. How can a book shock a person?"

"Odd, The first time I touched it, I got shocked, too, but I thought it was the shelves." Using the napkin, I picked up the small book and gave the cover a few quick taps with my finger. There was no shock, no pain, or anything like before. I ran my fingers over the lettering, hoping maybe it was metal and thus might have conducted some electricity. Yet to my fingers, it felt like any other old ink. Wrapping a napkin around it, I set it aside carefully. "Why would a book shock us?"

She shook her head, not accepting the explanation but unable to find a viable alternative. "That can't be right. It must be something else."

We looked in the book's direction, wondering what could have caused a jolt. But before we could ask questions or think about it further, a server appeared, ready to take our order. Asking for more time, we put aside the book's shocking feel for the time being.

"I guess we don't want to be touching it before a meal. No telling where it's been." For my repetition of her sage advice, she awarded me with a wadded-up straw wrapper aimed at my head.

As much as I wanted to talk about why a book was shocking, beyond plot twists, I remembered this was time with my fiancée and we still needed to eat. Once I was back at work, I'd follow up on the book and maybe learn more about its properties. It would probably be something disappointing, like batteries in the cover from a failed marketing campaign.

Settling back into the reason we came to the restaurant I checked the time. There was no need for us to rush, but with Alana's work, that could change in a moment. I gave Alana a concerned look. "So, what's on the agenda for the last half of your day? More tests? I know we are on lunch, but how fast do we need to get back?"

Alana sighed with a slow shake of her head, returning her attention to the menu. "There are more tests we can run. You can never have enough data before you begin experiments. But right now, all the equipment and parts are in the cleaner."

Giving her an understanding nod, I picked up the menu and noted my favorite meal was still there before setting it back on the table. "Well, hopefully it will work with no problems or complications this time." I reached over to give her hand a reassuring pat.

She smiled back, a hint of pain and concern in her eyes. She had worked for many years to oversee a large-scale project of this nature. The fact she was reporting her results to the CEO himself made accuracy even more important. From what I was told, she was working on developing an innovative new product. Even Alana didn't know what the data was going to be used for, only that nothing seemed to be enough. "There's no need to worry. It'll be fine. For now, let's enjoy lunch. What did you decide on?"

She gave my hand a gentle squeeze. "A chicken salad. It seemed like the healthiest option, and I'm kind of in the mood for chicken."

My mouth fell open in surprise and disbelief. "You mean the same thing you get *every* time? Ms. Kym, I am surprised at you!" I laughed, and she joined in. No matter what was coming for us, I knew we would get through it together. I wish I had known then just how bad things were going to get. Maybe then I would have asked for extra bacon.

Chapter 3: Wonderland Pharmaceuticals

After a lovely meal, which I still think would have been better with more bacon, we returned to work. As I did every time we arrived, I responded with a cheerful sigh of enthusiasm. Never once did I groan or whine about having to return to work after a heavy meal, especially not when Alana put the car in park. "Back to the grindstone. I wonder what exciting whimsical journey lies in store for the rest of my afternoon."

"Don't be such a pessimist," Alana retorted as she gathered her things. "We have good jobs and do important work. You should be proud."

"You have an important job. You work in the labs, doing all the cool stuff. Working in the back rooms is like being Quasimodo, just without the bells. I'm isolated, alone, and forgotten." Hunching down, I shambled toward the security door and did my best raspy voice. "The bells! The bells!"

Alana let out a cough, but I could hear the start of a laugh being squashed by professionalism. "Lab work isn't all glitz and glamour, you know. I keep telling you it's all about following the processes, thorough reading of instructions, and repetition."

"Repetition," I echoed, pulling on the door. Since I had forgotten to swipe my badge, the door refused to budge, and my shoulder ached at the resistance. "That's saying things over and over?"

Ignoring my remark, she continued her train of thought. "At least you get to walk around and see people." Getting her badge ready, she scanned us into the employee entrance and held the door for me. She looked at the book sticking out of my pocket. "Let me know what you find out, will you? Although I would probably not mention you took it out of the building. You could get in trouble."

"Catching me implies someone comes to my lair and doesn't just have me bring them what they want. Sometimes I wonder if I am the only one with access to the storage areas. Besides, it's not like I'd be reading on the job or anything."

She gave me a look of disbelief. "Who are you, and what have you done with my fiancé?"

"I'm Steven, and I pod-peopled him," I quipped back with my best alien-sounding voice. "You'll never see him again."

Alana gave me the start of a smile. "Well, trash day is Tuesday, and you're in charge of scooping the litter box." Her words trailed off with a small laugh.

As we walked through the office area, we passed a series of flat-screen televisions playing the company's latest commercial on loop. Images of the facility, the grounds, and groups of employees transitioned across the screen. On the bottom of the screen was a transcription of the commercial's script.

Wonderland Pharmaceuticals is among the most advanced laboratories for clinical trials and innovative testing. We offer state-of-the-art equipment. The pictures focused on lab work, which followed the standard image of people wearing lab coats and holding up vials to examine the contents, as if the naked eye could see the chemicals.

Here at Wonderland Pharmaceuticals, we believe every idea that advances humanity warrants exploration, and we work with our partners to be a leader in environmentally conscious technological breakthroughs, genetic research and modification, and treatments for every manner of ailment, both human and for our little friends. Stock photos came up showing people throwing a ball for their dog at the park, a very smiley woman with a bird perched on her finger, and a family looking at fish in a large aquarium.

Wonderland Pharmaceuticals is focused on advancing and improving the quality of all life for everyone here on planet Earth. Now, let us hear from our CEO, Vincent Payne. The video changed, showing a man in green scrubs that looked too crisp and clean to have ever seen lab work. On his head he wore an emerald green derby, another item that would never be seen in labs.

"Did you notice that they never have pictures of cats?" I mused as we stepped away just before the CEO's speech began. We had heard it a dozen times at least, and if you'd heard one corporate speech, you'd heard them all. Instead, I focused on our conversation. "All the stock images they have, but not one with a kitten."

Alana shook her head. "Yes, you've mentioned that... several times now. They probably can't get cats in the picture because they don't like fun or being playful. Plus, when is the last time you've seen a cat pose photogenically?"

"All the time! That's the purpose of the Internet. Plus, I know I could get Purloin to model. He's a fun cat."

"No, you couldn't. Purloin doesn't care about doing anything besides eating, sleeping, and biting your feet. I doubt you can get him to take part in anything that doesn't involve those things."

"You make him out to be a bad guy, but he always runs up to greet us when we get home. Besides, now I have a book on how to train cats... even if it has a lot of chemistry and equations I don't understand. I bet once I finish reading it, I can make Purloin a big deal. He'll be on the side of cat food bags all over the world." To emphasize my point, I made a sweeping gesture with my hand and ended up sending a rack of pamphlets scattering across the floor. A few people looked over, some of them laughed, and one let out a yelp. While I worked to clean up my mess, I could hear people whispering comments about me. Alana blushed and bent over to help me.

"Marcus," she hissed in an angry whisper. "We're at work. Jokes at lunch are one thing. We do serious work here." Before I could respond, she added, "Not everyone wants to be the center of attention." Handing me the pamphlets she had collected, she cast a glance at the onlookers, then looked away from me. "I need to get back to work." Without another word, she turned down a hallway leading to the lab's locker rooms and disappeared.

"Alana," I whispered back, knowing she would not hear me. My heart fell in my chest, and I headed down the stairs to my subterranean lair, away from all the surface dwellers who did all the important work.

Chapter 4: Quest Accepted?

Returning to my station, I found someone had picked up the stack of boxes and tossed the paperwork haphazardly on my desk. "Heathens! Has humanity lost all respect for a man's desk? Does no one use the inbox anymore?" If someone else were there, they might have laughed. Even Cartly didn't laugh, which, the more I thought about it, was probably a good sign for my mental health.

Removing the strange book from my fleece, I propped it up so I could see the cover as I logged back into my computer and began my research.

Database doesn't list it. Looks like all that's in here on the boxes was their numbers. Man, would it have killed them to put any information in the database back then? How was anyone going to know what was down here? It's like they wanted these boxes to remain lost forever.

A little pride sparked in my chest. Even if no one upstairs knew it, all the years I had spent down here updating contents might one day be useful to a future person in my role. *A forgotten hero to my successor.* My smile dimmed, and I changed my approach to investigating all the other boxes in the series. *If it's not in the box's inventory, maybe the titles of the contents will give me a clue.* However, all that told me was these were old records from the earliest days of the company.

Returning to the depths of the archive, I started going through any boxes that remained on the shelves, but all of those were generic scientific notebooks and blueprints on the building's original construction. Seeing the old prison overlaid with the plans for the manufacturing site made my blood run cold. Knowing it was an old prison was bad enough; seeing the remnants here and there was creepy, but those spots that got filled in to build on top of—

Shutting the last of the dusty old boxes, I shook my head. Something about being in front of an old prison cell, even ones that had not been used in decades, gave me the heebie-jeebies. It was like the world was hiding away a mistake, and my working here was all a part of hiding that old shame. Nothing good could come of that, although I comforted myself with the notion that I did not know what the right call would be.

In the end, all this trip through the dark history of the company did was confirm we had been in business for a long time. Many people had better lives thanks to the medicine and therapeutics we designed. Looking through old contracts and supply orders was not helping me find out anything more about books that could shock a person with a touch. As I walked back, I turned the idea over in my head.

Could there be something along the spine? Maybe put in to keep it all together and help it stand up straight? If it's hidden under the leather, no one would see it, but with as worn as the cover is, maybe a little piece of metal is poking out. That could create a spark.

Picking up the book, I ran my finger down the spine. It was firm, not as broken and battered as most old, tossed-aside books would become. I gave it a quick series of taps, listening for a metallic clang, but I was rewarded only with a leathery thump. No hint of a metallic clink or any reverberation came from the binding. Next, I examined it for any tears or gashes that might betray hidden wiring or a metal strip, yet despite the faded color, the book seemed to be in excellent condition.

So why did Alana and I get shocked?

The lack of an obvious answer was kind of exciting and my heart beat a little faster. This was a mystery for me to pore over, like the start of a quest in some old novel. Sure, it would probably end with some stupid defect warning saying they used a weird chemical in the manufacturing process, causing the covers to spark. But at least with that story I could bring it up to people as a fun bit of trivia.

As I set the book back on my desk, my phone buzzed. The reception in my area was terrible; all the concrete and steel above me normally killed cell signals. I reached for my phone, remembering that Alana had mentioned contacting me earlier. There was some generic update message on the screen, so I put the phone away and went back to my computer. Even if there was a critical phone update, there was no way I could connect to a network down here. It would just have to wait until I got home.

My online searches were equally unfulfilling. There were no mentions of electric shocks from books or any mentions of magical manuals for cats. Whatever the book was, it seemed to be unique or at least rare.

There were a few people at the company who might recall hearing about the book or rumors of older files, so I sent out some requests for confirmation. Since I wasn't highly regarded by anyone, I imagined they would refer me to the archive email group, which ironically, only included me. Still, it couldn't hurt to ask around.

As I waited for replies, I took a moment to stretch and checked the large analog clock. For all the forward-thinking innovations that Wonderland Pharmaceuticals employed, digital clocks were not among them. The owner seemed adamant on this topic but never explained why. The best hypothesis I'd overheard in the lunchroom was that Vincent Payne saw it as a metaphor for the old being integrated into the modern age. That the gears of time were always counting forward, even in the modern age.

Of course, that was all just rumor. I had only ever seen the CEO on the commercials in the lobby and at the occasional all-employee meetings we had at the launch of a new project. Alana had met him. In fact, her current project on regenerative tissues was something he had come up with. This was her big chance to impress him, but her success never seemed to be enough for the big boss.

Only three more hours to go.

A tiny beep went off, giving me just enough time to get back in my chair and look alert before the door swung open. I knew other people had access to the area—maintenance, security, and other higher-ups who had access to everything—yet seeing someone else come through the door was rare.

Two figures entered the room. One was dressed head-to-toe in an emerald green suit, with a familiar derby on his head. The other was built more like a section of living wall. The man in green cast me a wide smile, his teeth practically glowing against his dark skin and clothes. The figure behind him scowled. His head moved in a slow ratcheting motion as he surveyed the room.

"Ah, perfect! Just the man I wanted to see." Vincent Payne, CEO and owner of Wonderland Pharmaceuticals, beamed.

My mouth went dry as I tried to process what was happening. This wasn't just an intern dropping off another stack of things to file, a courier with a stack of boxes, or anyone delivering requests. This was the big man himself, appearing as if he had just read my thoughts.

In mere seconds, I would be in a conversation with someone important, and I was woefully unprepared. "Mister…" Vincent Payne drew out the last syllable, his head swiveling until he found the nameplate on my desk.

"*Magus* Kyle," he corrected, sounding slightly impressed. "Well, this is a fortunate day, isn't it, Solomon?" He turned back toward me. "Did you know, back where I'm from, a magus is a genius among men? That is splendid news for me since that means you'll be able to help me with something."

The thing behind him gave a grunt in reply, making me wonder if that was what passed for a laugh among walls. "Um, it's actually Marcus, sir," I corrected him, my voice not nearly as confident as I wanted it to be. Thankfully, it seemed he had something else on his mind and was not paying much attention to anything.

"That's great," he replied, ignoring my correction. I got the feeling he had already planned out what he was going to say before he arrived, and anything I said was merely background noise. "So, tell me, Magus, do you ever want to be involved in acquisitions?"

Clearing my throat, I stood a little straighter to show I was a competent and intelligent employee. "You mean orders, sir? I can place orders, but mostly I just get more storage boxes and supplies for the archive. I have access to the ordering database, but—"

"Fantastic," Payne answered, slamming a sheet of paper down on the counter. "I don't want to waste time going through a bunch of channels. See, I'm a direct man. I like to go to the source of things. That's why when I needed my boxes, I sent Solomon here to collect them. I'm sure the form had something generic written on it, but I really couldn't wait for it go to from department to department before it would finally be delivered to me. All that red tape and bureaucracy just slows down actual work."

The thing he called Solomon stood nearly seven feet tall and had to crane his neck to not scrape the ceiling. Built like the son of a quarterback and a wall, he bumped into shelves every time he made even the slightest motion. But somehow, despite his bulk, he inserted himself between me and Payne.

No one at the company knew anything about Solomon. Not where he lived or where he was from. His qualifications were easy to see: he was a misshapen thing that loomed over Vincent Payne like a gargoyle on a cathedral. What made him more even unnerving was the aura of silence around him. The dull hum of the old lights quieted, and the whistling vents went still. It was like the world around Solomon held its breath in the hope it would not catch his attention. Not only had no one ever heard him speak, but the way he moved and shifted without making a sound was the stuff of nightmares.

I suppose when you are looking for a personal bodyguard, big, intimidating, and staying quiet are good qualifications. Why Vincent Payne needed a bodyguard in a secure facility made no sense to me. If anyone had ever asked why, I had certainly never heard an answer. That I had just missed encountering him earlier sent a shiver down my spine. I had no desire to be alone with that beast.

Snapping back to the moment, I realized Payne had been talking. "Well, anyway, since you got me everything I need, I figured maybe you could help me find something else I've been trying to get my hands on for years."

"I'd be happy to help find anything you want, sir. I apologize if the boxes earlier were a bit banged up. My cart broke—"

"You hear that, Solomon? This man is working with broken equipment." Payne made a snapping motion toward Cartly. The colossal figure reached out and snatched up my cart with one massive hand. Even though it was just a thing of metal and rubber, I had a pang of regret for my two-wheeled companion being hefted by the towering figure.

"We will make sure you get a new one. But for now, on to

what I need you to help me find. This is for a personal project I am working on. I'm taking the company back-to-basics." Vincent Payne walked around the stone archive as if he were on a stage, his voice echoing in the distant, dark corners of the room. "Sometimes you must step back to see the bigger picture, see where you came from to know where you're going. Now, after all this time, I'm finally ready to take the company in a new direction. This new project is going to be game-changing, young magus."

There was an intense look in his green eyes, passion and excitement, a flash of anger and a raw energy that drew me in. "What I am doing will change the world. Everything the company has been working on for all these years will look like a children's science fair compared to what I'm doing next. You get me?"

"Sounds great," I mustered. "If it's all that important, shouldn't I go through procurement? I mean, they can expedite—"

He shook a hand in my direction, dismissing my words as if they were fluttering around him. "No, I'm a busy man and I can't spend all day waiting for forms to be completed or meetings to be held for cost analysis. All the usual red tape. You know how verbose we get here. It will be too late by the time I get what I need. I've already set things in motion, and I believe with what you provided me earlier, I can proceed." With a flick of his wrist a small, folded piece of paper appeared between his fingers. He extended his hand towards me with the poise of a practiced stage magician. "Please."

There was a raw power behind his words that shook me to my core. Nothing would make me happier than following that command. That force of personality, that charisma, must be why the Payne family had been in business for so many years. You just could not say no to a man like Vincent Payne. "Order this for me and get it here quick. I'll owe you a favor."

Taking the crinkled paper, I read it over. There was the name of a chemical, a company, and a quantity. "Okay... I mean, this shouldn't be too hard. Let me check our suppliers and see if we have an account with—"

Another object landed beside the list, a platinum credit card. "No need. Just put it on my card." Vincent Payne leaned on the counter, getting uncomfortably close to my face. "I really need this to be kept hush-hush since it's for a top secret new line of products. Understood, Magus?"

Nodding again, I picked up the card. "I can do that, sir. You can count on me. Consider it done."

"Good." He bobbed his head at me. "You've got a real future here, Kyle. It's good to know there's a man down here with a good head on his shoulders." Vincent Payne leaned against the counter beside my desk as pride welled in my heart. The head of the company was here talking to me and giving me an important job. It wasn't the labs, accounting, or any other department getting credit; it was the man who was the lowest both in terms of physical location and ranking on the corporate ladder. This was like something out of a dream. Before I could say anything else to convey my appreciation, his eyes fixed on something on my desk.

"That's interesting," he said and reached out to snatch the red book from my desk.

"Wait," I called, hoping to spare him an electric shock. My hand extended to stop him, but he had been too fast for my warning. Solomon bristled, drawing a breath that made it feel like all the air was being pulled from the room. I flinched back instinctively.

"Something wrong?" Vincent Payne replied, holding up one hand to ward off the massive figure while he looked at me.

"Oh, it's just I thought you might get shocked."

He shot me a glare, and our eyes locked. His eyes were a deep emerald green, and the playful glean he had earlier was replaced with a sharp, hard edge. A I looked at him, I became acutely aware of my surroundings. This was an old prison's lowest levels, now a concrete tomb for forgotten books and files. There was no one else on this floor, no one came down here, and I was alone with two powerful figures. One, the CEO who ran this place. The other, a silent slab of granite with tree trunk sized arms and legs. If anything happened to me here, who would believe me over either of them?

Unsure why my comment caused the energy of the conversation to shift so quickly, I backed away. I had only taken a single step before I was against the wall. The hair on the back of my neck rose, and I cast a quick glance at my phone. I doubted I could get any signal. Maybe the landline? Even if I made a call, who could help me?

Vincent Payne stalked toward me, shaking the book at me as if warning me to consider my answer. My mind flashed to a documentary that depicted a wolf advancing on its prey. "Shocked?" he said in a slow, even tone. "Were you shocked by this book,

Magus Kyle?"

"It… it's just kind of strange." I coughed; my throat parched. "But it's so dry down here. Sometimes you get a shock touching stuff."

Payne held me in his sight for a moment, then chuckled. "Of course, that makes sense." With one hand, he flipped through the pages before letting out a full laugh. "Well, I can see why you think it's strange." He threw the book back to my desk without looking, sending a stack of papers scattering to the floor. "The thing is blank. Probably really confusing for archiving, right?"

"Blank?" I repeated, recalling all the images and inscriptions I had read earlier.

"So anyway…" He laughed, his demeanor flipping back to a jovial tone. A moment earlier I thought I was a dead man for trying to warn him. Now he was acting like we were old friends sharing a secret. My heart raced, and my hand trembled. Imagine me, Marcus Kyle, a nobody in the basement, talking to the CEO like equals. Let me tell you something: that moment was electric.

"Can I count on you for my order? I need it as soon as possible." He paused, leaning in close. "For *my* work."

With a slow nod back, I wondered if this was one of those character tests HR liked to set up. Still, saying no to the owner of the company was probably just as bad for my career as doing what he said. True, this was not the usual process, but the entire premise of our work was to break limits and challenge paradigms. Would I really want my only interaction with the owner to be that I said no when asked to do my job? This might be my only chance to get any kind of recognition and be more than just a stock room guy.

Looking Vincent Payne square in the eyes, I gave a firm bob of my head. "Of course, sir. It would be my pleasure."

"Good," Payne growled in contentment. "See, I knew you were a smart man, Magus." He used the title again and looked over his shoulder at the larger man. "Didn't I tell you he would be a team player, Solomon?"

Solomon grunted out a sound like concrete blocks rubbing together, but otherwise he made no move to acknowledge the comment.

Vincent Payne looked me over, as if he'd finally deciding I was an actual person and not a piece of furniture. "Good," he repeated. "You know, I like you, kid. You have got gumption, spunk, and smarts in equal measure. I'm sure you'll go far here." He turned, taking a few steps toward the door before adding, "Let me know the second you get my items. I'll send Solomon to pick them up. This is paramount to my research and to the advancement of my endeavors."

"Just remember, it's all hush-hush and need-to-know. Only you, me, and Solomon"—he stopped to point at the intimidating figure— "know about it. So that means only two of us would ever talk about it."

There was a hint of that earlier malice in his last words, an easily implied threat. With Solomon forming a protective barrier, the two stepped out of the room, and the man in green smiled. "Be seeing you soon, Mr. Magus."

"It's Marcus, sir." But it was too late, and my name echoed in my archive room.

At some point, I had sat down, and the aftermath of an adrenaline rush hit me. For the first time in as long as I could remember, someone important had given me the responsibility of doing something that mattered. The resonating sound of my voice was almost like a crowd cheering me on.

A war of emotions nearly made my heart burst. This had to be the biggest moment in my life, and I was riding a high of excitement; I'd been in the presence of the big boss, and I couldn't wait to see what succeeding could mean for me. But at the same time, I feared the repercussions that failure could bring. A small voice in the back of my mind questioned why this project was so secretive and what was going on with the look Vincent Payne had been giving me. However, I brushed it off as the eccentricities that came with being a big shot.

Everything else fell away as I started on my mission. This was my chance, and I would let nothing stop me from placing his order.

Chapter 5: mRecombinant

Vincent Payne's handwriting was neat and exceptionally fine, as if he was used to writing on the side of a grain of rice. Eventually, my eyes focused on the tiny script and I deciphered the name of the company he wanted me to find. *It's like he's whispering the name to me with writing.* Below the company name, he had written 'week's supply needed', but he failed to specify how much was needed. Hopefully the company's website could provide order quantities and might explain what would make up a week's supply.

The order was for mRecombinant. *Recombinant... Is this for some kind of cloning or genetic testing? That would be major and might tie into Alana's regenerative project.* A wave of new excitement filled me as I thought about how my new project might even let me help Alana. I could be a hero on two fronts.

Wonderland Pharmaceuticals has a database of over one hundred suppliers we do business with. I've lost count of how many times the procurement department boasted about their network at our company meetings. However, there was nothing in our database that mentioned anything about mRecombinant. *Perhaps it's too new to be in the database?* I admit, seeing a gap in the system made me smile a little. It was nice to see the people above could make mistakes and weren't as perfect as they considered themselves.

Since our system didn't have the answers I needed, I turned to my favorite internet search engine, Yohoogle. My grin broadened as I mused on the idea of finding what I needed using an everyday tool. *Score one for the underground dwellers.*

Things did not go as smoothly as I had hoped. The first few pages of results were for various recombinant chemicals, but not what I was looking for. The search engine kept trying to autocorrect my query, and more than once I vented my frustration with the changes it tried to force on my phrasing. Finally, after eight long pages of results, I found a website for a company called Moebius Materials that had mRecombinant in its description.

Moebius Materials' website looked like it had been created when the Internet was young. The last time someone updated this site must have been the early 2000s, when flashing banners, stocky columns of data in Comic Sans, and spinning logos were cool. The page background was an ancient-looking castle, and at first, I thought I had accessed an old video game or role-playing game site. It was a unique choice for a corporate website. At the top of the page, a red and yellow banner read *Recombining in Time*. On each side was an animated trumpet that seemed to announce that I had entered the website. As I scrolled down, fiery sconces flickered and led me back to a set of double doors with the word "enter" written in an archaic font.

Chuckling, I clicked on the doors and began my quest for the materials. Navigating the site was more of a game than a normal shopping experience. Every click became a test of nerves and luck. With the age of the site, I could easily envision it crashing if I clicked the wrong thing or made too many choices too quickly. Of course, there was also the possibility I could download a virus onto my computer. *Our firewall wouldn't let me on this site if it wasn't safe, right?* Confident I was on the right track, I continued to delve further.

The first challenge was figuring out how to navigate. Instead of text, a corresponding image accessed every link and subsite. A book icon led to an archive of compendiums with a page heading that read *Alister's Albums*. That name made me pause. *Alister? Like the book? That must be a coincidence, right?* I made a note on some scratch paper to come back later and investigate this part of the site when I had more time. Right now, I was on a quest for a holy relic called mRecombinant. With it, I would bring peace and glory to my homeland of Wonderland Pharmaceuticals. The bubbling beaker took me to Gallows' Glass, where flasks and other glassware was for sale. The link with a Tesla coil sent me to Esmeralda's Equipment, which not only had old lab machinery but also an assortment of cooking utensils, camping implements, and tools.

While each subsection shared the same level of basic construction, it was as if I was walking through a marketplace with various vendors calling out for my attention. Each had their distinct establishment and products.

Clicking icon after icon, I eventually found a corked test tube that led me to Payne's Potions. *A test tube, really? A beaker would have made a lot more sense. Also, why is it called Payne's Potions? Does Vincent Payne own this shop? With as much money as he has, I would think he could afford a decent website. Then again, if his site was easy to use it might show up on the corporate radar.*

My mouse swung between the vial icon and the option to shut the page down completely. Tension built in my shoulders, and I tapped my foot on the floor. It would be easy enough to just close out and go back to searching. Or I could just tell Mr. Payne I wasn't comfortable buying from this site and wanted to clear it with him first.

Playing out that scenario in my mind, I saw Mr. Payne give me a nod of confidence, wearing a wide, toothy grin as he listened to my report. "Do what seems right," he would say. "Isn't that right, Solomon?" He'd snap his fingers. The lumbering brute would step forward and—

Cutting off the vision, I brought myself back to the moment. *It wouldn't go down like that*, I chastised myself. *All that would happen is I'd let down the big boss and lose my chance. Maybe get fired later if it turns out what I've done is terrible.* Still, the towering image of Solomon loomed in my head. Someone that size probably chased kids down beanstalks on his time off.

With a final, sharp inhale I steeled my nerves and clicked on the icon. A new page came up showing a road closure sign that read *Closed to through traffic.*

Never in my life had I been so happy to fail. If the website was down, no one could fault me for not being able to place the order. Letting out a raspy wheeze of relief, I moved to close out the page and try my luck again. However, as my mouse traversed the screen, the background flaked away like a scratch-off lottery ticket. The more I moved, the more I saw.

After a series of quick strokes, I uncovered the treasure buried underneath: an image of a lion standing on its hind legs and facing left. It reminded me of something you would see on an old flag. Underneath the image was the first link that used words. My sigh was a combination of confusion and curiosity that trailed off into relief as I read the long chemical name. Like all chemicals, it was a mix of numbers and letters, subscripts, and superscripts. Whoever had designed the web page must have really been into specialty fonts, because random letters and numbers twirled and jumped back and forth. *On the one hand, I can appreciate the showmanship and zany nature of it. It's quaint, for its time. But on the other hand, how the heck do they expect people to order anything from this site?*

Clicking the link, I looked away long enough to get the credit card. But when I tried to move my mouse again, nothing happened. The screen froze. "No, not now," I begged, clicking in rapid succession, fighting for any response. With a heavy heart, I prepared to restart my machine. This would mean losing all the work I had completed, and there was no way to be sure this would not happen again if I came back to this site.

Before I could complete the shutdown, a simple gray window popped up with a question and a space for answers. The lettering was all in small caps and italicized.

WHO ARE YOU?

Stopping myself from restarting, I smiled. "Okay, just lagging. That's not too bad."

As soon as I answered that question, another appeared:

DO YOU HAVE THE PROPER MANUAL?

As I considered this question for a moment, the red book on my desk caught my eye. *That's right. This was from Vincent Payne's boxes. I bet the manuals were in there.* Again, I gave my answer and received more questions. My groan echoed off the stone walls. "Pop-ups…"

HOW WOULD YOU RATE OUR WEBSITE ON A PRECAMBRIAN SCALE?

Before I could reply, and long before I understood, a larger window appeared. This one was more elegant, with a font that looked like handwriting.

We apologize for the frequency of our questions. As this is your first time visiting our site, we realize this can be very disorienting. Please bear with us and provide the proper responses. This is to ensure maximum safety. Once the questionnaire is complete, you will return to your regular performance. To start, please enter the quantity desired.

What was up with this site? *Maybe it's just old and glitching while trying to run everything. The smart thing to do is close the browser and contact Mr. Payne to let him know the product is not available. After all, I was tricked by a book's cover earlier. Do I really need to prove how gullible I can be again?* Taking a sip of water, I read the statement a few more times and whispered to myself for reassurance, "I won't get bamboozled again."

Would you like to continue?

Every alarm bell in my head went off, warning me to step away and move along. Folding my hands so I could touch the mouse, I stared at the button. *If Alana were here, she would walk away. She'd know this is all too out there and would play it safe.* I could almost hear her saying those exact words in my ear and imagine how easily she could dismiss something like this as nonsense. Freeing my hand, I moved to close the window. This time there was no secret hidden message or resistance. *It had all been part of the act to get me to screw up.*

My heart raced, and I lifted my finger to finish the order. The thought of Alana being proud of me for my decision gave me strength and the resolve to push forward with my plan. Yet just as I was about to close it out, the scenario with Payne and Solomon played out again in my head. In this version, Alana stood beside me. That memory brought a smile to my face, and I knew we would get through anything together. But the scenario changed. Instead of looming toward me, Solomon shifted, heading to Alana.

If I don't do this, and Alana supports me, they might take it out on her. My hand slid back to the center of the screen. If I did this, maybe I could use the good favor I won with Mr. Payne to help Alana. I could be a hero.

That was when I clicked the okay button. After that, things passed in a blur. I honestly don't really recall all of what I answered. Maybe it was fear, excitement, weariness from thinking about it all too much, or some combination of the three, but I just started typing as fast as I could. It was almost a game. Answer the pop-ups before the next one showed up. It was like I had two different questionnaires going at once. Some were in the handwritten font, and were about chemical knowledge, how dense the packaging should be for the item in question, how long the experiment would take, and purity of the substance. I answered to the best of my knowledge, but felt my stomach drop when I submitted each answer. Not knowing the project's scope, I could only hope I was doing the right thing.

These were intercut by the strange all-caps font asking me about my opinion on the website, its color palette, and the sound files it used. As my area made every sound echo, I kept my laptop muted, and could not answer that last inquiry.

SORRY TO HEAR THAT YOU CAN'T HEAR IT.

With the way the comment was written, I could almost hear a goofy laugh following it. I continued answering questions until a question came from the handwritten font.

Almost done. Please enter quantity.

"Finally," I sighed in relief, "I need a week's worth… so I guess that would be at least seven." No sooner had I entered my response, than I received an error message.

Quantities of 8 only (maximum of 8).

"Why even give me the option?" Correcting my error, I confirmed the amount and continued answering questions. Now that the handwritten font was up, it asked how fast I wanted the package to arrive. The options were more images, each one depicting a different stage of the sun's path across the sky. They set the first to high noon, the second at sunset, and the last was just a black box.

Selecting the middle option, I prepared for the worst part of any online order: payment. It was one thing to answer questions and such, but I was dreading the point when I had to enter Vincent Payne's credit card number. I had already submitted to the madness of playing with a probable virus, but now I could be financially impacting Payne as well. Yet no questions about payment appeared. Instead, a window popped up.

THANK YOU, MAGUS KYLE. WE HAVE CHARGED YOUR CARD. CONFIRMATION WILL COME SOON. PLEASE HOLD ONTO THAT SLIP.

That upset me. It was kind of funny when I made the joke about my name being like the old sorcery title, and I imagined Vincent Payne was calling me that to butter me up so I'd help him with such a weird task. But I knew for a fact that I typed my name in properly at the beginning.

As soon as I cleared away that window, I returned to the homepage. However, now none of the links responded. As I shut the page down, a last pop-up appeared.

Sent to the printer.

My printer whirred to life, spitting out a confirmation page written in what looked like hieroglyphics. All I could understand was a single line: *DELIVER TO MAGUS KYLE.*

This entire process had been surreal. I've used difficult websites before, but never had to answer so many questions. It was like I had been through an audit and could only hope I passed. What confused me was why the webpage's designer used two different fonts for the questions? Why set it up in a series of pop-up questions like a conversation instead of a simple form? I supposed that was why the website was so obscure. No one in their right mind would put up with a website like that.

"Still, at least they got my name right for the delivery, but—"

"Marcus," a woman's voice chimed. My heart nearly stopped, and I may have squealed like a cornered mouse, as I turned to see Alana standing at the door. "Geez, Marcus, it's only me," she added, a look of concern in her eyes. "Are you alright? Why haven't you answered any of my texts?"

"Huh? What texts?"

She sighed. "Have you been messing around all day again? Let's go."

"Go? Why? What's the emergency?"

She held her phone so I could see the screen. "No, it's time to go… You know, home."

Returning to the moment, I checked the clock. "Wow, that order took a lot longer than I thought."

Alana's face brightened. "Order? Please tell me it was for work. We have enough stuff piling up at home, and you don't need to be starting any weird new hobbies."

"No, it was a work order. Nothing weird at all. Just helping." I trailed off, remembering Vincent Payne's request for discretion. While I would consider Alana an exception to the rule, now was not the time to test that hypothesis. "Helping," I said, leaving it at that. "I just need to finish shutting down, and I'll be ready."

"Okay then." Alana nodded. In her eyes was a hint of pride I had not seen before. Was it something I said? Maybe something I was doing? Whatever it was, I liked it. Maybe she was in on this order, and this was all part of some corporate test. But that seemed

too far-fetched. Plus, Alana was both a terrible liar and bad at acting.

"I'll meet you at the car." She yawned. "I've been on my feet all

afternoon and need to sit down for a bit."

With a final click, the door closed behind her, and I started

shutting down for the weekend. When I reached for the small red

book, I stopped. Was it okay for me to take it home? Vincent Payne

did not seem to have any interest in it. He had called it blank. That

part had really confused me. Was that some business slang for

"useless"? Earlier, I looked through it and had seen plenty of writing

and images inside.

Opening to the middle, I gasped and began flipping through

the pages as fast as I could.

Every single page had gone blank.

Chapter 6: Ride Home

Alana put the car in reverse and started moving the moment I opened the door. Throwing myself into the seat, I got situated and fastened the seat belt on the fly. "Geez, Alana. What's your hurry? Can you give me a few minutes to get situated before we go street-racing?"

She grunted, pulling out into traffic as I attempted to retrieve everything I had dumped on the floor. "We've been here long enough today." There was a sting in her voice, a barb of agitation behind her words, and it made me flinch.

"Everything okay?" I was hoping her earlier grumpy nature was because of our leaving in the middle of a project, but now she seemed tense. A twitch was forming at the edge of her eyes, which was a sure sign something bad had happened.

She shook her head. "My project is finished. We wrapped up all our work and the results looked positive. It seemed like the cellular regeneration was up by thirty-five percent, but when I took the results to Mr. Payne, he didn't seem to care. It wasn't just that he didn't care about how big of an increase this was. He actually seemed bored by it, like I was wasting his time even being in his office. He said the entire project was being scrapped as they prepped for actual work. Something about the timing being right and that he needed to get ready. He told me that my results, while he was sure were impressive, were not what he was interested in. I'll be going back to my old station on Monday. No more project ownership for the time being. In one conversation I went from leading the biggest new project to back running data reports." Letting out a long, sad sigh, Alana took another sharp corner. "Right now, I just want to go home, take a bath, and try not to be too discouraged."

"It's been a busy day." My mind was racing. I had so many things I wanted to say, to talk to Alana about, but was this the right time? She *was* feeling down. So my news about my special project with Vincent Payne might cheer her up, or it might just sour her mood even further. Telling her about all my research yielding nothing and the fact that our boss didn't get shocked when he touched the book and that the contents were now blank probably wouldn't help.

"Look, I'm sorry about earlier," I offered. "I know you aren't a fan of being the center of attention. Especially with all that's going on at work."

Alana shook her head. "It's fine. I shouldn't have snapped at you like that. You were just trying to make me laugh. I'm just a little on edge with my project. I really thought this was going to be a big deal. I mean I don't do this job for recognition, but it would be nice if the big-wigs would at least talk to me like a person and give me some constructive feedback or direction instead of an abrupt end."

Nodding as she spoke, I waited until she paused to let out a long sigh before I replied. "Companies. Can't talk to them and can't burn the whole thing down. At least not legally." Alana chuckled, the anger in her eyes from the day's events fading away just a little. "Also," I added, "did you really say 'big-wigs'? After calling me out on using 'flim-flam' earlier?"

She let out a full laugh, "at least my word is something people use in this century. Yours sounds like you're going to try and sell me some snake oil."

Now we were both laughing. As she drove on, I looked at my phone. Besides all the missed texts from Alana, a message had appeared on the screen. "Upload complete. Make this device default?" There was an option to either accept or decline.

What upload? Does it mean update? My finger hovered over

the options. After the daunting experience I had with that old website earlier, I was in no mood to mess with strange pop-ups. Clicking decline, I checked my apps and files for any changes. Nothing appeared to have been altered, so I relaxed a little. The last thing I needed was some malware messing up my phone.

Another pop-up appeared. "Original restored. Updates pending approval."

"Something's weird with my phone," I muttered.

"Well, don't keep clicking on things," Alana yawned, the day's weariness seeping into her response. "We can take it in tomorrow, and have it looked over if we need to."

Setting it aside, I picked the book up off the floor. No shock hit my fingers as they made contact, and I flipped it open. I realized it might not have been a good idea. If Alana looked over, she might notice the blank pages. That could cause her to be distracted while driving.

"Gah!" I screamed before I could stop myself, causing Alana to swerve.

"What?" she snapped back, giving me a sideways glare. "Are you hurt? Do you need me to pull over?"

"No, the book. It has words in it." Confusion choked out my words, preventing me from explaining further as I turned through the pages, seeing that every picture and word had returned. *Wasn't it blank earlier? Did I imagine that? But why did Vincent Payne see it as blank? Were there just a lot of blank pages in the book? Was that what I'd seen?*

We drove in silence for a full minute before she spoke. "Marcus, dear, I love you, but that was *not* funny."

"Sorry," I whispered, staring at the page. "I must just be tired. Stress and all. It's been a weird day." Turning through the pages, I hoped for a section that might still be blank. Just two pages was all I needed to prove that I was not crazy.

One thing I loved about books was the simple joy of turning the page, of seeing what adventure was in store on that other side. Yet this time, each flip stoked my anxiety. A cliffhanger as I searched for confirmation of my hopes. I probably would have gone through the entire book on that car ride, but one page caught my attention. I had not seen it earlier, but I had only flipped through it briefly this morning. While the rest of the book had been written in black, the ink here was an electric blue, giving a sheen to the letters, which sparkled like a gemstone. The title at the top of the page said: Recipe for Recombinant Alpha Tonic.

My interest piqued, I read over it multiple times. The chapter described this experiment as a simple potion for realigning energies, a good place for beginners and people starting from scratch. It was an exercise that could increase the skill of the practitioner. The explanation for the theory behind how this worked was referenced in an appendix, and some entries pointed back to earlier topics. However, this seemed simple enough: mixing a few items and stirring. Some details focused on timing, specifically how the best time to make this tonic was called "the Witching Hour." Stuff like that always made me laugh. Why would the time-of-day impact how chemicals reacted? I supposed it was a sign of the times when superstition ruled more than sense and science. But still, a part of me was drawn in. The book itself was a mystery, delivering electric shocks and seeming to sporadically become blank. I wanted to know more, and maybe trying out a randomly blue experiment would be a good way to learn more.

The instructions went on for several pages, explaining theories and making comments pointing to other chapters containing additional information. Sometimes it even pointed to other books in the series. Could those be in the boxes Mr. Payne wanted? Did he know anything about them? The more I thought about it, the more questions I had, and I forced myself to focus on the main instructions. "I'd like to try this recipe."

Alana gave me a patient smile, her tone calmer after I had been sitting quietly for the last few minutes and not randomly screaming about words in books. With the way she spoke, I could tell she was trying to be positive, despite her own situation. "Recipe? Is it a cookbook now? I thought you said it had chemistry equations and that it was supposed to be about cat tricks? Now that I think about it, why did you take that from work? Did you find out anything about where it comes from?"

"I couldn't find anything about it online or in the database. I was told it was not important." Clearing my throat, I promised myself I would explain it all in more detail in the morning once we calmed down and relaxed. "'Recipe' seems to be what they call experiments and potions in here. It has all kinds of equations and theorems. Funny, I always thought that was a word for an idea."

She rolled her eyes at me. "A theorem is a proven result.

You're thinking of a theory, or rather, you're thinking of a hypothesis. It's just all those movies and video games you play use the wrong word."

"Makes sense." I nodded in agreement, but I am sure the vacant look in my eyes betrayed my lack of understanding. A faint hint of a smile cracked her dour expression. "In any case, this is probably the weirdest book I've ever read. I will give it this: it hasn't been boring, but it's just… strange. Each time I read it, I find some fresh surprise." Closing the book, I looked over the spine and binding. There were no obvious signs of damage, nor did it look like the cover had been replaced. Not that I was an expert on bookbinding, but I'd owned a lot of books and I liked to think I could spot a repaired book.

"This recipe looks pretty easy. I don't know a lot about chemicals, but some sound really familiar." Throwing my head back, I gave the car's floor a kick. Things clicked in my head. "This is a joke book!"

"While I think you shouldn't take it seriously, nothing you mentioned sounds funny."

"Not like that. I thought maybe it was a gag gift, but maybe that is what it is. *It* is the gag." Burying my head in the book, I took a deep whiff before coughing at the musty old scent of ancient paper. "The smell has faded, but I bet this is written in lemon juice or some kind of disappearing ink, only appearing in daylight." A weight came off my shoulders as realization washed over me. "It's all part of a joke. This is just a bunch of junior chemistry experiments. That's why Payne was acting so weird."

"Payne? As in our CEO? Why do you think he was acting weird? What happened today?"

"Well, you said he wasn't interested in your report," I said, still not comfortable talking about my interaction, now out of embarrassment that I was part of some gag. *I bet that's why they didn't need the credit card. This is probably some prank they pull on the guy in the archive. Still, that means I was tricked again by a book.* With my personal crisis averted, I looked over at Alana, who took a moment to look my way as we turned, making sure I wasn't having some kind of panic attack or mental breakdown.

A thought came back to me. If it was all a prank, what… what about the blue page? If it was a disappearing ink, why was it so different from the rest of the pages? As I thought about it, the solution fell apart. It was like my brain was fighting itself, trying to distract me with random guesses, but I was too stubborn to just go along with it.

Finally, I tapped the blue-inked page. "Even if it is fake, it might be fun to try it out this weekend." That little voice in the back of my head told me to toss the book out the window, to just forget it all and move on. Go home, play video games, read any of my other books, and just relax. Do anything besides fixate on this one random book. The feeling was telling me that this was my last chance to step away and pursue my own goals.

Alana laughed, and my growing concerns and fears faded back in the depths of my mind. Hearing that sound always made me feel better. "I'm glad you're interested in chemistry. We can look when we get home. We just need to be safe and do it with plenty of light in a well-ventilated area. I imagine…" She continued describing ideal laboratory set ups. While I could hear what she was saying, she moved through the steps needed in rapid succession. I honestly couldn't keep up and hoped she could explain it again when it came time to begin. Since setup was out of my depth, I turned my attention to the blue instructions on the page, reading over them in a constant loop.

"This book gets more complicated the more I read it. Alana, you took chemistry in college. Does it ever get any easier or start making sense as you read it?"

"As long as it isn't organic chemistry. No one really understands it." She laughed, a piece of her dour expression falling away. "Many people leave the field at that stage. It's a genuine test of character and commitment." Shaking her head, Alana drifted back from the tributary memory and into the flow of our conversation. "The whole point of a textbook would be to provide basic information and get more complicated as it goes along."

That piqued my interest. After all, I wanted to start from the beginning. *Starting from scratch, what could possibly go wrong?*

Chapter 7: Home Sweet Home

We live in an old complex with a nice courtyard. It was a quiet place, outside of the hustle and bustle of Savannah's day-to-day activities, but still close enough we did not have to spend large parts of our days driving to and from work. Everyone at the complex kept to themselves. The only ones who really interacted with us were the cats and dogs in the courtyard. Not only was the area pet-friendly, but there seemed to be an unwritten rule that everyone could have an animal of their own.

Alana unlocked the door and a cacophony of noise greeted us as something large crashed its way through the house. Stacks of books, which I really intended to read one day, toppled over and piles of papers spilled onto the floor. Cords were pulled from sockets, and something fell with a crash that would require a dustpan and broom to clean. Her face darkened as the destroyer appeared, slowing from a racing white comet to an almost dainty prance.

Before us sat a large white cat with golden amber eyes. He had long, wild fur and the biggest ears, paws, and tail possible on a house cat. Yawning, he licked his lips before giving us a coo mixed with his meow.

"Purloin." Alana sighed, as she stalked in the direction the shattering had occurred. "What did you get into this time?"

Unlike my fiancée, I bowed low and scratched behind Purloin's ears. "Hey, buddy. How was your day, Purloin?" He meowed in response to his name. While he never reacted to anything else, saying his name always earned me a meow. "That good, huh? Lots of birds and squirrels out there who now know you are the boss?" Purloin flicked his fluffy tail, signifying the conclusion of his greeting ritual. He padded toward the kitchen, stopping after a few feet. He looked back at me and meowed. When I did not immediately move, he trotted back and sat down to stare at me. "I know, I know. You want dinner, right?"

Alana came into the kitchen, holding a broken ceramic figurine. She sifted through the junk drawer until she found the superglue. Purloin strode before her, accepting her wicked glare with cool indifference. "Purloin, I wish you wouldn't get up on things. There are breakables on those shelves."

"He's a cat. They climb. Maybe if we let him out in the courtyard, he'd be calmer by the time we got home. We could install a cat door."

With a steady hand, Alana held the broken arm of the figurine in place as the glue set. "Yes, but would you actually let him outside? You worry about him enough as it is, and he's never been around other cats or dogs. What does he know about protecting himself? As big as he is, Purloin is just a house cat. He's no lion, Marcus." Purloin meowed in response to his name. "Yes, I'm talking about you, troublemaker."

It was an old conversation, one we revisited often. No one ever seemed satisfied by it, so I decided now was the time to shift to something new. "Okay, so what about my experiment? Do you think we have the stuff to run the test?"

Alana looked at me over the top of her glasses, easily seeing through my attempt to change conversation. "Hold this." She nodded to the broken arm. "I'll go upstairs and check our junk room. We should still have the chemistry kit you got after that superhero movie. It's probably still unopened." We traded off on the holding of the arm, like we were exchanging a golden idol for a bag of sand to prevent the jaws of a trap from activating.

"It's not a junk room. It's storage," I called after her. "I'm going to finish every project up there. Then I'll start all the unopened ones. It just needs to be organized."

"Where would you even start? The costuming sets, old electronic repair kits, your book-binding supplies, or maybe all those old cookbooks?"

About a minute after Alana had left, I could feel the glue taking hold. Moving a saltshaker close enough to hold the broken piece in place, I flipped open my red book and began going over the experiment's list of chemicals. A pinch of salt, a dash of baking soda, some talcum powder, and a variety of other things. Opening every cabinet drawer and inspecting every shelf in our refrigerator, I started pulling out anything that had an ingredient related to my hunt. Eventually, I discovered it was easier to just grab everything and sort it out later. It was like being a kid in a candy store, but instead of sweets, I was hunting for powders and liquids.

Upstairs, something shifted and collapsed. "I'm okay." Alana coughed. "Just moving your projects into smaller piles."

Every step of the way, Purloin followed, sniffing at every single item I found. He meowed in disappointment when I moved potential food away from him. No matter what I was doing, he was a few steps behind me. It had been that way since he was a kitten.

When I found him—or rather, when he found me—he was a small kitten who I tried to move out of the road. He hid in my car's undercarriage and rode home with me. That had been a day to remember, and sometimes I thought about how much could have gone wrong. Since that moment, we'd been inseparable. If I got a snack, he hunted for the crumbs. If he got into a tucked-away space, I'd fished him out after he got stuck.

"Well, I braved the depths of the vault, and I found an old chemistry kit," Alana proclaimed with triumph as she held up a faded box. "I doubt any of the chemicals are still worth using, but the test tubes and candle could still—" She froze, staring at the results of my scavenger hunt. "I was upstairs for *five* minutes," she whispered. "How did you turn the kitchen into… into… *that* in five minutes?" Before I could respond, Purloin leapt onto the counter, the crowded space causing him to bump into the saltshaker and knock the figurine's ceramic arm free.

"Talent and teamwork," I offered, hoping she might just laugh it off. Just like before, my attempt failed. Alana often said I did not stick with things, but here I was, still trying to nudge her mood toward laughter.

"Marcus," Alana warned through clenched teeth, sliding the old kit onto the counter. She let out a long breath to calm herself down. "I'm glad you're getting into chemistry—again—but could you please not destroy the kitchen while doing so?"

"Sorry, Alana," I offered in my friendliest tone. "I'll clean it all up. Why don't you go take a bath and relax?" She set the chemistry set down on the table, eyeing the growing assortment of ingredients with concern. "Maybe I should look upstairs, see what I can find?"

She scanned the room, surveying all I had accomplished in such a short amount of time. "No, then you'd just make a mess in another room. How about I go look, and you get dinner started? There should be something in the freezer."

Purloin let out a grumble, stretching until his head bumped my hand. "Yes, and I'll feed you, buddy." Placing the prepared bowls aside, I grabbed Purloin's bag of treats and dropped a few into the bowl to tide him over while I went upstairs. Purloin gave a half-hearted growl to dismiss me as he consumed his snack with ravenous hunger. Backing away to give him his space, I started getting dinner ready.

While I was no chef, I could pre-heat an oven and cook a frozen pizza. As Purloin chomped and the oven beeped, I looked at my phone. A notification showed that my tablet and phone had synchronized, and I could now look at the photos of my new book on a larger screen. Before I could start my research, someone knocked at the door.

Purloin looked up from his bowl but did not slow the pace at which he consumed the last crumbs of his treat. He looked up from licking the bowl and gave me a look that said, *get rid of them*, and continued chomping. Neither Alana nor I was expecting anyone, and it seemed too late for any deliveries.

Peering outside, I saw a van pulling into our parking area. On the side, it had a large lion logo that reminded me of that website's icon. "That must be coincidence, right? I mean, a lion is a pretty common mascot…" Another knock came from the door and I jerked back.

Cracking the door, a small man holding a wrapped package stood waiting. He wore a top hat with a lion logo. He smiled broadly as our eyes met. "Package for you, Magus," he said with a cheery tone.

"Um, my name is Marcus Kyle. I think you may have the wrong person." Just before I could close the door, he leaned forward, and the box bumped me back.

"No mistake, sir. You placed an order for some chemicals. Here you are." He thrust the package forward, forcing me to take it. Before I could protest, he stepped away. "It was a pleasure to meet you, Magus Kyle."

Confused, I brought the package inside and unwrapped it on the dining room table. Inside were eight vials with cork stoppers, their contents a shimmering rainbow of colors. The insides moved like a lava lamp, blobs drifting in their suspension. "What in the world is this?" There was an opalescent quality to the liquid, color sparking along its surface. For a moment, I thought back to the vial I had found this morning and left on my desk. *I wonder if it's the same goop in each one, just separated by decades.* Setting the vial down, I shook my head to dismiss the thought. If it was the same chemical, why would Vincent Payne need me to order it? After all, something that had been around for so long should not be that hard to find. It could be an old chemical that was no longer carried by most distributers, or maybe Payne didn't like the thought of people at work knowing he was trying out something so archaic. The idea of mixing up random chemicals to see what happened, and throwing in some old-school stuff for good measure, appealed to me. I could certainly see the excitement in that idea. Maybe Payne and I were not so different after all?

Having resolved the notion, or at least provided myself enough of an answer that I found it boring to continue that line of thought, I started searching the padding until I found the invoice and confirmed that the chemicals were for the recombinant solution I ordered earlier.

"Who was that?" Alana called down the stairs.

"Delivery guy," I responded, turning the paper over in my hands as I tried to figure out what was going on. "But it looks like the package I ordered at work got delivered here."

"Were you ordering more books on the job?"

"No. This was something they asked me to order for a project. But it makes no sense why it came here. I put in the company address and everything. Nothing should have listed our place. Plus, I ordered it a few hours ago. There is no reason it's here, and I don't understand how it got here so fast."

Alana peeked her head out from the stairs.

I pulled a vial from the box and showed it to her. "There are no instructions, and I am not sure if this needs to be refrigerated or not."

She shook her head. "I've never seen a chemical like that. What is it supposed to be?"

"It's mRecombinant," I answered, hoping that it would be enough information.

"That doesn't make much sense. Recombinant is just the recombining of an organism, cell, or genetic structure. It's not a kaleidoscope of colors and blobs."

Purloin took that moment to jump on the table, spilling some ingredients I had pulled from the kitchen onto the floor. Unconcerned with the mess he had just made, he meowed with indignation as he looked in the box. Full boxes that didn't have the decency to contain food were among his greatest disappointments. Any empty box was the only kind that he assigned any value, as those he could sleep or play in. He batted one paw at the insulation, testing to see if it might hold the potential for amusement.

"I know you're hungry," I told Purloin, removing him from

the table and earning myself a series of furious complaints followed by a loud grunt. "Just a little longer, I promise."

As I gathered up the strange chemicals, I remembered how insistent Vincent Payne had been about getting this package. *This could be my chance. If I got this to him today, I might really impress him. Plus, I have no clue how stable this stuff is or if I can legally even have it here. Maybe he could explain what exactly is going on. I mean, none of this fills me with much confidence.* "This could be my ticket to being important."

"Meow." Purloin gave me a flat, uncaring reply before looking over his shoulder toward the kitchen.

"Hey, Alana. I'm going to run this package to work. No clue why it came here, but this way, no one complains about the shipping." Grabbing my keys, I hefted up the box and started toward the door. Purloin complained again. "Please feed Purloin," I called out before racing out the door.

The whole way back to work, I tried to figure out what I would say when I met Mr. Payne. Would I tell him the package came to my house? Should I play it off as if it were no big deal? Was now the time to talk about Alana and my potential in the company? I mean, all those corporate training seminars talked about seizing opportunities and being your own salesperson. But would this be too much of a slight detail to focus on? All I was doing was delivering eight vials of weird-looking liquid to the CEO.

I made it to work in record time, only violating a few traffic laws along the way. As I pulled into the parking lot, my head swiveled side to side in search of Vincent Payne's car for a full minute before I realized I did not know what his car looked like.

You're putting the cart before the horse again. Alana's voice came to mind, echoing all the previous times she had warned me about doing that exact thing.

After parking with haste, I snagged the package and ran to the entrance. The door refused to open, and I patted my legs, looking for my badge. "Where is it?" I groaned before realizing it was still in the car. Just as I turned to head back to my car, the door swung open. "Oh, good." I sighed. "Thanks, I forgot my badge, and—"

Solomon's bulk filled the doorframe. He glared at me with a cold and unfeeling expression. His eyes lowered to the box in my hands. My body shook at the low rumble that emanated from his chest.

"This is for Mr. Payne," I offered, flipping open the box to show him the contents. His eyes opened ever so slightly, and he might have made a gesture that a statue would consider an attempt at a smile. "It's really a funny story. You see, Alana– she works in the labs— and I had just got home when—"

The large man's hand lunged toward the box. The sudden motion caused the words to catch in my mouth, and my stomach dropped somewhere near my ankles. Anyone looking at me probably would have seen my soul leave my body as I recoiled from the larger man. Never in my life had I seen anything that big move that fast. All the movies I'd watched really did justice to what it was like. His arm ratcheted back, all of the vials grasped in one large hand.

Solomon emitted another growl, and he stepped back into the building. The door swung closed behind him. "You'll let Mr. Payne know that Marcus and Alana got those for him, right? Solomon? Buddy?" My only reply was the click of the door shutting. "Okay," I shouted, talking more because of nerves than to be heard. "I'll talk to you on Monday, big guy."

Walking back to my car on wobbly legs, a rush of emotions hit me. Fear at the silent, tall man. Anger that I had been so easily dismissed. Confusion at what was happening. Disappointment from having really tried, and still it didn't matter. I sat in my car, taking deep breaths until I could get my nerves under control.

"What was all that?" I asked myself. I'd been dismissed and ignored before, but something about that interaction really messed with my head. The empty box sat beside me, and I could make out the tag on the top. I read it aloud to myself: "To Magus Kyle, never stop learning what you already should know."

Starting the car, I shook my head. "Tell me about it, Boxy. Let's go home."

Chapter 8: Gathering Ingredients

While I made significant progress in calming my nerves on the drive home, a part of me was still uneasy. I had seen Solomon walking around the labs before, with his grim expression and that monstrous stride of his. People always commented on how much he looked like some wild animal more than a human being, but I never paid it any mind. Yet I couldn't put aside how much his presence had unnerved me. The way he disregarded my mere existence and took those vials without a word. When it happened, I thought I just hated being ignored, but the more I looked back at that memory, the more I hated how small and weak it made me feel. Under his eyes, it was as if I shouldn't even be alive.

Alana was sitting in the living room and caught that look on my face. She was on her feet before I could say the first word. "Marcus, what's wrong? What happened?"

I tried to speak, but words would not form. Instead, I let out a billowing sigh and let my hand point aimlessly around the room. When I finally got enough of my nerves under control to speak, I blabbed out a mostly coherent reply. "Ran into Solomon. That guy. He just... Well, he freaks me out. I feel like a bug about to be squashed." I stopped, a shiver running up my spine. "When I opened the door, he was *right* there. Didn't even say a word as he took all those vials. I guess they knew about the mix-up. I'm not sure how, but they must have figured it out."

"It will be okay," Alana told me, pulling my head to her shoulder. "I'm sure they know it was all a mistake. No one is going to be mad at you for a shipping error."

"I guess so," I mumbled, my face still squished into her shoulder. "Do you want to start the experiment? It's a simple intro potion called Onlucan Gleawnes, and its mostly just colored smoke. It sounds funny, but it says, 'If you do this potion, you can do anything in this book.'"

She laughed in her quiet and soothing way. "I think we've had enough for one night. It's been a long enough week. I think it's time for me to go to bed. You coming?"

"No, I think I'll stay up and play on the tablet. Maybe review the book a little more." I held up both items. "My brain's moving too fast for me to sleep soon, anyway."

"Well, don't stay up too late." She yawned, walking toward the stairs.

Purloin hopped up beside me, making a gurgling meow as he rubbed against my leg. "You are a different cat once you've eaten, aren't you, Purloin?" He let out a sharp exhale in reply, almost like he acknowledged what I was saying.

The download to my tablet was complete. In fact, I discovered there was even more content on my tablet than I had expected. Not only did the photos transfer, but it also had a full electronic copy of the book. *Did I download a digital copy? How did that happen?* I turned the paperback over in my hand. There was no QR code or barcode anywhere on the cover.

Just as I cracked open the book to continue searching for an explanation, a window popped up on the tablet's screen, reading, "Make this copy your primary? YES or NO."

As I did with any pop-up, I clicked YES and opened the book. The animation of the cover opening was well done. The screen zoomed in and there was a rustling of pages and the audible crack of an old book's spine. The animation settled on the first page.

Under normal circumstances, I preferred paper over electronic copies. Yet even I had to admit the quality of the font and the clarity of the diagrams was far superior. It was like I was reading a brand-new copy of the book. Some sentences that I could have barely made out earlier were now written in a neat, understandable fashion. There were even a few lines I didn't recall reading before. "Weird. It almost looks like there are more lines in this version than my copy. Maybe there was a revision?"

With a flick of my finger, I went through the pages, looking for any copyright information or anything that might talk about any updates or publishing information. When nothing came up, I grabbed the paperback to compare it. Once again, the book was blank.

Immediately, panic gripped my heart as I tried to determine what I could have done to make an entire book get wiped clean. Purloin became alert as he sensed my distress, rolling back onto his stomach and looking around the room.

"This makes no sense," I whispered to calm myself. "Accepting a digital copy doesn't destroy the paper version. That's not how anything works."

Realizing my panic was for something mundane, Purloin returned to his nap and let out a displeased grunt.

Going back to the tablet, I verified it still had a copy of the book, then went to the instructions for the experiment I had been prepping earlier. I was pleased to see it all remained, although it now contained two new sentences.

FOR ADDED EFFICIENCY, ADD THE CHEMICAL UNDER THE TABLE TO THE CONCOCTION. ALSO, LIKE ALL GOOD MAGICAL EXPERIMENTS, THIS POTION IS BEST MANUFACTURED DURING THE WITCHING HOUR.

"Oh yeah, because that explains so much," I grumbled, petting Purloin with my free hand until he rolled onto his back and let out a slow, rhythmic purr. His relaxation ebbed into me, calming the growing agitation I was feeling for this book.

"Now all I need to figure out is what any of that means. What chemical under the table? Is that a mistranslation?" Something was off about these new sentences. The choice in font reminded me of the pop-ups on that weird website I had used at work earlier. But that idea seemed too coincidental. I was probably just tired, and my brain was creating random patterns to stay alert.

Before I could delve on that that topic any longer, the page on the screen flipped. I realized I must have been fidgeting while I thought and accidentally moved on in the book. I saw the answer to some of my questions on the new page before me. My heart tensed as I read the lines. The font was different now, looking like the handwriting style I had also read earlier.

Now, Magus, I am sure you have questions. Questions such as, "What chemical?" and "Witching Hour, what is that?" For the former, please look under your dining room table. You dropped something earlier. As to the latter, the Witching Hour, also called the Devil's Hour, is a time of night associated with supernatural events. It is when magic is at its height. If you have ever been up late at night, you may have experienced this phenomenon. There is a stillness to the world, as if everything on Earth is waiting for something to happen. This can occur between the third and fifth hour of the new day, at least two hours before dawn breaks.

You may think this text is reading your thoughts, but please be assured, we all have questions like these, and they were taken into consideration when the initial book was penned.

"Okay, this is too weird." Putting the tablet back on the charger, I decided it was time to call it a night. There had been enough weird occurrences and coincidences for one day, and I was probably just imagining everything happening. My overworked and overstimulated brain creating links that didn't exist.

Purloin let out a happy meow as he raced to his bowl, sitting before it in anticipation. "Nice try, buddy." I laughed, reaching down to scratch his ears. "I know Alana fed you, and you already got sympathy treats from me, so your sad eyes won't trick me this time."

As I stood back up, a glint of something under the table caught my eye, and the book's comment about a chemical came back to me. Reaching under it, I plucked one vial that must have fallen out of Payne's package. *How did this get here?*

Purloin huffed, displeased to no longer have my full attention and that I was not putting food in his bowl. He leapt up onto the table, shoving many of my containers closer to the edge. "Did you knock this off, Purloin?" Instead of answering, he merely sniffed the vial and rubbed his face upon it. "This isn't food," I instructed while moving it away from the table. Like before, the strange colors and blobs inside demanded my attention. There was something strange about this chemical, and my tired eyes watched as it drifted back and forth within the golden solution.

"It's too late to be running this back to work. I guess I'll just do it on Monday. After all, they didn't seem to care earlier." Securing the vial between some old flasks and bowls of materials, I went to bed.

Chapter 9: Experimentation

Sleep did not come easily that night. I tossed and turned trying to get comfortable. When I finally drifted off, images of the book's pages and that strange, entrancing chemical kept coming to the forefront of my mind, waking me. Such instances were not that uncommon with me, although normally it was a new video game or a book that would get into my head and would not let go until I solved the current mystery. Still, in those situations, I could at least force myself to fall back asleep. This situation kept growing in intensity, with a building sense of urgency. My heart rate picked up, and a bead of cold sweat rolled down my cheek.

"Marcus," Alana groaned in a half-asleep voice. "What's wrong?"

"I can't sleep."

"Purloin or video game?" Alana asked, shifting to regain her comfortable position. "Did you feed him? I forgot."

Grabbing my phone, I checked the time. "I didn't. I thought you were going to. But it's already 2:00 a.m. If he isn't waking us up now, he will soon." I gave her a quick kiss on the forehead and got out of bed. "Be back soon. I'll feed him and do some more reading."

She rolled over with a moan of agreement, closed her eyes, and slipped back into a peaceful sleep.

Purloin greeted me at the bottom of the stairs with an energetic squawk as he made his way to his food dish. His head dipped, mimicking the motion of how he would normally eat his meals. He regarded me with his amber eyes, a look of anticipation at his coming feast as well as his frustration at the delay.

"My bad," I offered, going to the jar holding his food and scooping out a portion of kibble. "I know you expect more from your servants. I hope you'll forgive us, my lord."

With a fierce intensity, the cat devoured every bit of my offering, licking up crumbs as if they were the sweetest ambrosia. By the way he ate, you would think we had never fed him before in his life. Purloin was a big cat, being partially Maine Coon, but despite his royal protests, I can assure you we fed him well and at consistent intervals.

Now that I had corrected my previous error in the eyes of the house's true master, I sat at the table to calm my mind. The Witching Hour described by the book was approaching, and I was compelled to do something, anything, to get rid of all my nervous energy.

The small flasks, bowls of chemicals, and the vial all rested on the table before me. "Maybe organizing this stuff will get my mind off things?" Unplugging the tablet, I stared at the home screen for a minute as I looked at the red book icon. "It's just a book," I told myself. "Nothing to be afraid of. You were just riled up from everything else going on today. That's all." Sadly, being convincing was not one of my skills, and I took a few more minutes to muster my courage before I opened the book.

A little WELCOME BACK! icon popped up, and I might have gasped before remembering that a lot of programs had that feature.

"It's just a book, Marcus," I said again, this time trying to put more confidence into my voice. Maybe if I sounded self-assured, I would trick myself into believing I was in control of the situation.

As I reviewed the ingredients and instructions for the better part of the next hour, I relaxed. Organizing and storing things had always been a kind of passion for me. I was never that guy who put a label on everything, but I always knew where or how to find something. I guess that made me a good fit for my job, even if it was as fulfilling as stuffing an envelope. There were a few items I had missed earlier, chemicals that sounded familiar, and the act of researching them calmed my mind.

Realizing these components would not be found in the kitchen, I headed upstairs to my storage room. The room was actually a second bedroom, but over time I started putting more and more 'on-hold projects' in there as I moved on to new interests. There were many great ideas in here. I bet any of these could change the world. If I only had the time, energy, resources, and money to complete them.

Sifting through my past endeavors, I found a set of homeopathic chemicals and a large jar of pickle brine. To be honest, I still don't remember what I had originally thought I would use the homeopathic items for. I think I just liked its ornate wooden storage container and the tiny jars that came inside it. Still, some jars had things I needed. The brine was from the time I tried out pickling various vegetables. It turned out that not everything tasted good pickled. The jug was heavy, and I could barely get it to the bottom of the stairs without dropping it. At the kitchen table, I fought down my desire to retch as I scooped out some of the liquid.

With these items added to my assembled chemicals, everything seemed in place. I set up each material in the order it would be added. All that remained was to start the process. Despite the heavy lifting, I was renewed, energized by the accomplishment. A smile crept onto my face. This was as close to "doing science" as I had come since I was in high school. I wondered if this was how Alana experienced every new project.

The idea of creating a potion from an old-looking alchemy book made me giddy. This was like something out of a fairy tale or a comic book. The moment where the wide-eyed kid took his first step into a magical world. Of course, I was no kid. I wasn't even an unpopular teenager in high school. I was a young man with a nine-to-five job and a fiancée. My life was mortgages, not missions. Doing something like this, even if it was all pretend and would probably lead to nothing, was my chance to try out something. Plus, since this was all from a book in a pharmaceutical building's archive, I was sure nothing bad could come from it.

When I had come downstairs, I had hoped to wear myself out and prevent a feline uprising, but now I was waking up and wanted nothing more than to continue. If I could not sleep earlier, there was no chance I could sleep now.

"What's the harm in trying it out?" I asked Purloin, who had begun a long bathing ritual. He cast me an offended stare. Clearly, I had broken some cat protocol by speaking during his routine.

"Step one," I whispered as I kicked off my experiment, since my audience of a bathing cat and sleeping fiancée did not seem to enjoy being disturbed by my grand experiment.

The steps went quickly as I added a pinch of this here and a dash of that there. Alana had mentioned that some chemicals were so old they might have lost their efficacy, which was fancy chemist talk for "expired like milk." However, I was determined to see this through. I wouldn't let something as simple as old materials stop me from conducting a magical experiment from an ancient book. Where would the logic be in that? Besides, this was supposed to be an introductory potion that would let me do any other experiment. Why not try it out really quick? Then we could do a real run tomorrow once Alana was awake.

Everything went smoothly until I got to the last instruction. This was one of those additions that had happened after I moved from paperback to electronic.

"Add the recombinant," it instructed.

Holding the vial before me, I looked down at the bubbling liquid. Every other chemical was mundane, either something from the pantry or the thing a store would sell to a student. But this stuff, this weird lava-lamp-like material, felt different.

As I popped open the top, a series of scents wafted over me. There was the scent of the deep woods, followed by the dry fragrance of a wheat field and then a metallic taste of blood. My head swam as I processed these smells.

Purloin stood, resting his front paws against my leg as he extended himself toward the vial. His nose moved a mile a minute, and he meowed a demand for whatever I was holding. He was determined to know if it was either a treat or toy.

"No, not for kittens!" My words did nothing to dissuade him as he pawed at my hand.

"Marcus." Alana yawned, suddenly descending the last few steps. Her voice was as close to a shout as a whisper could get. "Do you know what time it is?" She paused for a fraction of a second before adding, "It's three in the morning. You should be in bed. You can play lab tech tomorrow."

"Sorry, Alana." My voice returned to a normal volume. She shot me a look, and I matched her tone. "I'm almost done. I just need to add the last chemical." Holding the new chemical forward, I let a little bit of liquid within the vial slosh about and catch the faint light. Its contents sparkled, causing little reflective rainbows of lightning to crackle over its surface. "I just couldn't sleep and thought I would do a trial run. Besides, it's been a lot of fun, and—"

"Marcus," Alana groaned, still a little groggy. "Go. To. Bed. It's too late to be conducting experiments. You have all weekend." Her eyes turned to the chemical I was holding. "Wait, I thought you took all those back earlier. Where did that come from?" Purloin continued to whine, propping himself on my leg as he eyed the vial. Whether it was a treat or toy, he clearly demanded a chance to inspect and sample its contents. "If you were going to be doing a strange experiment, you should at least open the windows." She stepped off the stairs and into the room, unaware of the pickle brine jar. Tripping over the heavy obstacle, she lunged forward just as Purloin's patience wore out, and he dug his claws into my leg to propel himself toward the vial, determined to claim his prize. With everyone in one place at one time, my hand slipped from the vial, and the full contents poured out into my mixture.

The concoction issued a loud thump, and a thick blue mist rose from the glassware. It reminded me of the fog that dry ice machines made, only it was a sapphire blue. Purloin hacked, leaping away from the acrid-smelling smoke. He smacked into Alana, and the distinct crackle of static shock filled the air. In a flurry of fur and fury, he darted upstairs, seeking a hiding place. Alana coughed as she took in a lungful of the strange cloud and staggered toward the window. She unlatched the window's lock, but then wavered, went limp, and crumpled to the kitchen floor.

My own lungs ached, and my head swam as a fit of coughing overtook me. I had taken in a full breath of that strange vapor and my senses were going wild. Tears poured down my cheeks, my breath was hot and painful, and my skin felt fuzzy. Each hacking breath sent jolts throughout my body, like I was trying to spit out a lightning bolt. Struggling to my feet, I staggered toward the window and Alana. We needed fresh air, to get out of here as fast as possible. My thoughts were getting fuzzy, and there was a screeching in the air, like when a kettle reached its boiling point.

The next thing I knew, I was on the kitchen floor, my body

too weak to react. Strange thoughts came to my mind as I lay there. *I should shut that off before it wakes Alana... Purloin's probably panicking...*

Darkness filled my vision, and I drifted off. Whatever thoughts had kept me up earlier no longer forced me to stay awake.

In that last moment of consciousness, a disdainful voice called out in my thoughts, and one word heralded me into the darkness.

Dumb.

Chapter 10: Cat-a-Tonic

The next thing I remember was waking up sitting at a table. While the world came into focus, I could just make out the clinking of plates and silverware as they were being placed around me. As I worked on sitting upright, a voice called out to me. The speaker's tone and cadence were songlike, and the sentence ended on a high note. "Ah, you're awake. I was wondering if you would join me today or *non*."

The first thing I noticed was that I was no longer at home. I had expected to wake up on my kitchen floor or maybe in a hospital room, since I had passed out from the strange fumes, but I found myself in a small French café. Across from me sat a woman dressed in an outfit that was a fusion of mime and Halloween décor. Her makeup was done in a skull motif, but it had whimsical patterns of color, creating a border to her face.

"Are you talking to me? Where am I? Who are you?"

"*Bon*, the brain is working. You are with me, Mademoiselle Mina, and you are in my café." Pouring out two cups of tea, she spoke with a giddy energy. "I will do my best to answer everything. Oh, it has been too long since I have had a proper guest."

Her joyful expression and mannerisms eased the growing panic in my chest. Perhaps this was a dream. After all, I had just inhaled a lungful of chemicals. Maybe if I played along with my dream, I would wake up quicker. "This is a nice place you have here… very comfortable."

"Thank you," she chimed. "Being between places can be a frustrating experience, but being between moments can provide clarity. I find my little café quaint," she answered, finishing one cup and pouring the next. The scent was more flowery than I remembered tea being. "Now, you have some questions. Before I can answer anything, I need to let you know the rules of my café."

My stomach twisted a little at that comment. *Rules for drinking tea and talking?* "Miss, I don't think I'm supposed to be here. I have to get home. There might be some mistake."

"No mistake," she cooed. "I found you in need and invited you in."

"Where is here… exactly? The last thing I remember was mixing some chemicals."

She nodded as I spoke, seeming to confirm that things had happened exactly as I described. "*Oui, oui.* Now you are transitioning from your life."

"Transitioning from my life? Like dying? So this isn't a dream?" She said nothing in response but gave me a small smirk as she stirred sugar into her tea. Whatever game she was playing, that was a step too far for me to endure. "Okay then," I muttered, "time to be going."

"Without even getting your questions answered? That seems a waste of an opportunity, *non?*"

Ignoring her, I stalked to the door, determined to get back to my life. Throwing it open, I stepped outside and into a blistering heat. Immediately, my body seized up. The light burned my eyes, causing them to become locked in a squint. What I was seeing made no sense. There was nothing outside the café. Well, that wasn't completely true. All I could see was an endless wasteland of broken ground and sand under a pale-yellow sky. Grit blew in the wind, stinging my unblinking eyes. The only thing that broke up the landscape was a small, weathered shack, worn down by years of exposure to this harsh environment; it stood in defiance to the elements. I tried to move, to make my way to the shack and get out of this painful heat, but my body would not respond. My eyes were dry from the biting winds, but I could not close them even to blink. No matter how much I struggled or strained, I just could not force my body to respond. For all intents and purposes, I was a statue in a wasteland.

A chill grew in my chest, slowly reaching out into my limbs and stretching the length of my spine. "I need to… I need to move. Why can't I move?"

The door to the shack opened. I tried to call out, to turn, to do anything besides stand there, staring vacantly. A woman emerged, her expression hard and angry. She glared at me like I was some mangy stray animal that had wandered here looking to steal food. Words were coming from her mouth, and she waved to shoo me away. I could not make out what she said, and I could not comply with her dismissal. All I could do was stand motionless in the blazing heat, watching the world shimmer around me.

Then something dug into my shoulder and pulled me backward. Even when I was under attack by some unseen force, my muscles would not obey my command to turn. The more I moved, the more my body tingled with the sensation of pins and needles.

The world's colors inverted like a photo negative. Then

everything went dark. Alone in an endless darkness, unable to move while something clawed into my flesh and pulled me backward, my stomach tried to heave despite my inability to move. Light flickered, a series of flashes that brought momentary illumination to the desolate scene. I wished I could have closed my eyes against the light, but as I moved, the speed of the pulses increased and I noticed that the brightness was radiating from behind me. *Or maybe it's coming from me...*

With that thought, the next burst of brightness flowed out. When the pulse touched the horizon, it climbed up the sky as if it was hitting a wall. The light pulse reached the edge of my vision before there was a thunderous boom and the entire sky shifted and shook. Constellations that I had never seen before formed. One was a great wolf's head, another looked like a squinting pair of eyes, and the last one appeared to a two-headed, multi-limbed figure. The stars making up the images flared until they popped like blown lightbulbs.

As the sky sizzled, spots formed before my unblinking eyes and I saw Earth sitting alone in the sky. *I'm on Earth... aren't I?*

The woman from the café's words echoed in my mind. "You are transitioning from your life."

I kept commanding my body to move, to stop sliding backward. However, it seemed to be all for nothing. My eyes remained locked on the Earth as a hole tore the sky open and comets of every color soared out. Their tails wove together into a net around the solitary planet. When the comets' paths were fully intertwined, the multicolored net pulled Earth toward the hole. Even though this had to be happening millions of miles away, I wanted to hide, to not be visible to the force behind this display. As if in response to my thoughts, the power surged, and a tendril of energy fired at me. A rainbow of celestial power shot from the heavens toward me, and I remained frozen in place.

With a jerk, the tugging force on my shoulder pulled once more and I toppled over to the ground. Instead of falling onto dry, broken ground, I found myself back in the café. "What in the world?"

Standing over me was the woman from the café. She smiled as she looked me over. "Not of your world, *non?*" Helping me to my feet, she brushed dust off me. "Perhaps now you would like that tea? I assume you have questions, yes?"

Sweat poured down my face, and I enjoyed the ability to wipe my brow. "Yes, please. But I think it's going to take more than one cup to quench my thirst."

She laughed. "Well, while Mina's Café is always welcoming and accommodating, I think we only have time for one cup." We sat back at the table, and I reached for my cup. Before I lifted it to my mouth, she reached out to stop me. "Remember the rules. For every question you have, you must take a sip of tea."

"Okay, Ms. Mina-"

"*Mademoiselle Mina, s'il vous plaît*" she corrected with a childish smirk. "I am the owner of this café. A quaint place between the land of your past and the next place."

My throat went dry. "So, am I dead?"

"*Non*... not yet. Just having a near-death experience. If you were dead, you would have been at my sister's place. You might have seen it just across the way. Best not to think about it, anyway. You'll end up there soon enough. Everyone does." There was a playful coyness to her voice. She seemed to enjoy the entire experience.

My brain was tired, and I was not sure I understood what she meant or if I was supposed to follow the logic, but I nodded and took a sip. Coffee or soda were my go-to drinks, as I had always thought tea was too weak and had a strange aftertaste. Yet this was sweet and sugary. "What's in this?"

Mina squealed with delight. "First question! It is a home blend of herbs. Just a touch"—her voice spiked at the word— "of honey and no added preservatives."

Taking another sip, I decided not to waste the next question on something simple. I was getting tired and running on fumes. If it was a game we were playing, then I'd show all my cards. As you probably guessed, I'm a terrible poker player. "What is happening to me?"

"Your mind is too active. You stepped into a place that is on the cusp of everything and nothing. Now your brain doesn't know what to make of it. You should meditate on this. That is the wonder of rest. We see things that were, that were not, and many possibilities and impossibilities."

"Yeah, that really tells me nothing. You are telling me I'm nearly dead and I just saw Earth being dragged into a black hole by rainbow energy comet ribbons. Just saying that sentence out loud must mean I'm insane."

She said nothing, but a small smirk came over her face. Her eyes drifted from me to the centerpiece. A crystal globe filled with small glass beads. With one small hand, Mina reached into the container and picked up a single piece. She set it back down before repeating the motion.

I drank half of the remaining tea, eager to learn more and a little disappointed that it was almost gone. "That is good," I muttered. "So what do you think the vision means?"

Mina continued her repetitious motion and smiled at me. "You poked a hole in the world." Her playful laugh fell flat. "You've changed the entire world with your meddling. Whether that be for the better or worse, no one can really say. As for your next question, they are safe. At least as safe as anyone can be now." With that, she dropped the glass bead one last time. As it clacked against the others, I flinched and closed my eyes in reaction.

Chapter 11: Up!

When my eyes opened, I was still laying on the ground. *What was in that tea? Why is the tile so rough? Wait… are those stars?*

Up! A shrill voice commanded, causing the word to echo in my head. Strange images flickered in my mind. I saw myself in bed in the early hours of the morning, just before my alarm would go off. Then I was napping on the old armchair. The last vision showed me sitting in front of my computer. The angle of these scenes was the most unsettling. It wasn't from my perspective, or even how I thought I looked, but as if someone was following me and watching my every move. A primal fear of being preyed upon gripped my heart.

Up! The command came again, followed by the same images once more. The voice was angry and blunt. No, it was more of an agitated disappointment than anger. This time, there was a tugging on my chest, like an invisible hand was trying to lift me but was not strong enough.

Up! The voice in my head boomed a third time, with those same images, which now repeated on an endless loop. There was a deep agitation in the voice this time, like how my parents would give me a final warning when I was a kid.

Finally, with a wince, I sat up and took in my surroundings. Powerful hands grabbed me and pressed me down onto my back. A face donned with a surgical mask appeared in front of me and started speaking. It was then I noticed the ringing in my ears, as it blocked out everything the person was telling me. The figure kept repeating whatever he had said before, shining a small flashlight into my eyes. I winced at the sudden brightness but tried to keep my eyes open and follow his back-and-forth motions with the light.

What's going on? Wait... if I can't hear him, who was talking earlier?

After a few deep breaths of chilly night air, the fuzziness in my head cleared and the ringing subsided. Time seemed to speed up, at least enough for me to recognize my surroundings. The first thing I noticed was that I ached everywhere. Even while resting on my back, it was like I was lying on a pile of pins and needles. Every part of me tingled. The spots before my eyes coalesced into stars in a normal night sky, and I recognized the trees and building around me as our complex's courtyard. The figure looming over me wore a paramedic's uniform. He had been talking to me as I studied my surroundings. "What?" He leaned back from the volume of my question, and I realized the world hadn't gone quiet. I was still not hearing that well.

"I said, can you hear me, sir?" the man repeated in a calm voice.

After a few more calming breaths, my hearing was stabilizing. "Yeah. Yes, I can, sir. What's going on here? Where am I? Is Alana okay? Purloin, my cat, is he—"

Up! That same voice shouted in my mind again as a new series of images of me sitting and lying at home popped into my head, all of them from that creepy stalker's perspective. Again, I tried to stand up but was stopped.

"Sir, I'm going to have to ask you to remain laying. You breathed in a lot of… well, a lot of something. We think you're going to be fine. I'm going to need you to just stay down."

Dumb, the voice grumbled.

The whole thing made no sense. Someone was telling me to get up and calling me dumb, but the only one around was this paramedic, and he seemed adamant that I stay seated. If he was not talking to me, then who was?

"Marcus!" Alana shouted, running over to kneel beside me. "Thank goodness you're awake." My heart skipped a beat seeing her. I was teetering between relieved and terrified. She was draped in an emergency blanket and kneeled to give my head a quick kiss. I gave one of her hands a quick reassuring squeeze. "I thought you were—" Tears glistened in her eyes as she tried to find her voice. I nodded back to confirm I understood, and that I was okay, but tears started filling my eyes and it was hard to see if she understood my gesture. Another medic approached and gently led her back to the ambulance.

For the next several minutes, the medic examined me, and I followed all the instructions to his satisfaction, except for the continual command to stand up. Every time I tried to get up, he would remind me to stay seated. I wasn't sure why he told me to do something that he didn't want me to do. He checked my pulse, breathing, and just about anything else he before finally allowing me to follow the "up" command.

When I finally got up, I took a moment to let everything sink in. A crowd of neighbors had formed around me, only held at bay by a lone police officer. She barked a warning to anyone approaching and then continued writing in her notepad.

The hair on the back of my neck stood up. If the police had been called in, then they must have been in the house. What would they make of my impromptu chem lab?

No! That shrill voice boomed in my head, followed by images that almost made me motion sick. It was a series of first-person movies that included falling off the kitchen counter, running from a swinging hand that attacked as I leaned toward a plate of food, and accidentally pushed it off the computer desk. Some scenes were so familiar, and I got a strange feeling that I had seen these things happening before.

Just as the pieces were shaping into a picture, the officer approached me and cleared her throat. I gave her my best, friendliest smile, which most people said only made me look like a sick shark. She must have thought the same, as she took a step back before giving me the once-over. "Mr. Kyle, is it?"

Nodding, I shut my mouth to hide my toothy grin. *So much for first impressions.* I tried to remain calm and keep my head down, but all that did was add to my shifty appearance. Whoever said you should "act natural" in situations like this really needed to provide more details on what that meant. Otherwise, guys like me ended up acting like… well, like guys like me, and no one wanted that. Still, my shifting sights settled on her badge, where I could see her engraved name.

The officer flipped to the end of her notepad and loudly clicked her pen. She read over a few items before looking up at me. "Mr. Kyle, I am Officer Joan, and I have a few questions about tonight's incident. In your own words, could you tell me what happened here tonight?"

"Well, I was cook—"

"I spoke to your fiancée, Mr. Kyle," she warned. "Please don't waste my time by lying to me. You're in a strange enough situation as it is. Please explain what you were doing with those chemicals and lab equipment." Her eyes burned as she looked up at me, waiting for my answer.

Straightening my back, I tried my best to appear confident. "Well, Officer." My voice cracked as if I had just hit puberty. After a weak cough, it returned to an almost functional adult's tone.

The best way to describe how I answered is to tell you about the time I tried learning to drive a stick-shift car. My first few attempts to start the car ended with it stalling, as I could not master both clutch and brake at once. When I mastered using both feet simultaneously and could get the car moving forward, I stayed in first gear for several blocks, and the engine whirred as it struggled. After stalling at every stop sign, I got more confident and was able to shift gears easily. The second I got comfortable shifting, I downshifted when I should have gone up and heard the gears grinding in protest. In my panic, I looked away from the road and adjusted, only to realize I was going off-road and almost into a ditch. I swerved back onto the road and overcorrected into the far lane. Thankfully, there was no one coming, but if there had been, I would have certainly caused an accident.

The point was I was an idiot behind the wheel. "Well, Officer, I was conducting a magical experiment. I found an old spell book and wanted to try it out. My fiancée said I should wait for her, but I read that it should be done during the Witching Hour, and who knows when she and I would both be up so late at night? I mean, it's not like we'd wake up in the middle of the night to conduct an old experiment. Alana is nearly impossible to wake up once she falls asleep, and I'm way too groggy. I think it might have something to do with all the caffeine I drink, or maybe a lack of—"

"Sir," Officer Joan interrupted, breaking my rambling before I could get out every random thought bouncing around in my head. "That's enough, sir."

I went silent, my stomach twisting into pretzel knots. The thought of warm bread with salt became very appealing, and I had to tear myself away from the images of food to hear what the officer said.

"Sir, can I see your arms?"

"My arms?" Complying, I held my arms out, palms upward. Water started welling in my eyes; I had done it this time. I tried not to flinch as I prepared for her to cuff me. This was how it was all going to end, with me rambling about magic while being dragged away by the police. As terrible as that all sounded, I was more concerned about how it would look to Alana. I shot her a look over at the ambulance and found her looking back at me. I flashed a smile at her and hoped it was as reassuring as I wanted it to be. Joan shone a bright light up and down my arms, tilting the flashlight side to side, then grunted in surprise. Whatever she had been looking for was not present or not visible.

"Alright, well…" She paused, considering. "I think I have all I need, sir. But please, leave magic to the movies and games."

"That's it? I'm not under arrest?"

"No, but I'm sure your neighbors will have complaints. I don't know what you were really doing in there, Mr. Kyle. However, I plan on having some tests run on the residue from your nighttime experiment. So please don't leave town for the foreseeable future."

"That won't be a problem. I barely go outside, let alone out of town."

Our eyes met, and she glowered for a moment, considering her response. Then she reached into her pocket and pulled out a business card. "If there is anything else you want to tell me before the results come in, please call me at this number. It would be easier for everyone if you did."

Taking the card, a shock arced between us. "Sorry, I've been having a lot of problems with static lately." After a final shrug and one last once-over, Officer Joan walked away.

Police investigation, ambulances, and a chemical explosion going off in our faces… how unlucky could we be?

Chapter 12: You Can Talk!

"We are *lucky*," Alana fumed as she paced back and forth in the courtyard. "This all could have gone so badly. That the officer only gave us a warning and neither of us got taken in is a miracle. They could have charged us with arson."

"There was no fire, just some chemical smoke. Sure, it set off the fire alarm, but I don't think that qualifies as arson."

"I just know that we'll be getting complaints from the neighbors." She wiped at her eyes. "Why couldn't you just wait until tomorrow? What got into you?"

"I'm sorry, Alana. I didn't think it—"

"Exactly! You didn't think this through. I wasn't telling you to wait just to be a nag or boss you around. Honestly, Marcus, would it kill you to follow the rules just once? To think before you act..." Throwing her hands up, she stalked back to our home. I'm still not sure if I should have expected a better or worse follow-up conversation later on.

The stress of it all made my head pulse. I tried taking slow and steady breaths to stabilize my head, drawing in the cool night air. Inside, Purloin clawed at the door and I could just make out his muffled meows.

Images flicked across my mind at a dizzying pace, spinning and snapping in a frenzy of motion. The first was in the kitchen. I moved along the ground and looked up toward the counter. My stomach rumbled, and hunger on a level I didn't think was possible rippled through me. A long arm reached down and poured something into a bowl before me. I was so ravenous that I plunged my face into the bowl. All I wanted was to consume, to feast and end that terrible pain in my stomach.

When that scene faded, another slammed into the front of me. Now I was looking at Alana, who was eating some popcorn. One kernel fell from her full hands and landed on the futon. I raced over to the snack and bit down, chewing and crunching it down with excitement. The salty flavor danced on my tongue, and I was filled with the elation of victory. Finally, I saw another me sitting at the table eating dinner. From my vantage point on the floor, I tried to get the attention of my larger self, but he just dismissed the me on the ground with a wave of his hand.

Food.

The word echoed in my mind, the voice behind it agitated and demanding. Behind that anger was a feeling of deep offense, as if the voice were displeased at the mere notion that it had to make itself known.

Trying to shake the intrusive thoughts, the images continued to cling to the forefront of my brain. It was like having tiny nails poking out from inside of my skull. *Maybe the chemicals messed me up more than I thought. Should I have Alana take me to the hospital?*

Before I could process a response to any of those questions, another scenario took over my vision. This time Alana was yelling at me in a garble of nonsensical words. The pitch and tone told me she was upset, but I could not make out any of what she said. Her hand reached for me, and I remember being ready for battle but not concerned, as her pink claws weren't extended. She seemed incapable of extending them. Yet her strength was enough to tear my claws from my perch. *Claws? Why would I have claws?*

No, that same voice declared, resolute in its fear of seeing Alana. *Food,* it repeated, sending me the earlier images again but at a faster pace.

Placing my hands on my face, I tried to steady myself as the images pounded inside my skull. The pressure continued growing to the point I thought my head might crack like an egg. *What's going on? The paramedics said I was okay, but my head... Should it be hurting this much?*

Looking back at the apartment, Purloin was clawing frantically at the window. Despite the pain in my head, it was kind of nice to see someone so eager for me to come home. With one last deep breath, I headed inside. Purloin chirped with excitement as he raced to his food bowl, nodding toward it.

More images surged into my mind, followed by that shrill voice. This time it was excited and happy. *Food!*

"Where the heck is that coming from? Who's talking?"

Purloin ran to me, rubbing against my leg with encouragement, then returned to the bowl. It was like he was trying to remind me where to go. His meow was one of urgency and insistence. He sat back down and wrapped his tail around his paws, giving me the look of a displeased monarch.

"Yeah, I get it. You're hungry. You're always *starving,* Purloin. That's not exactly shocking news."

Reaching down, I scratched his head. Purloin seemed pleased

by my affection. I took some pleasure in seeing him happy, although it felt like more than that, as if someone was also showing me appreciation.

New images and sensations washed over my mind. First, food scraps were tossed down to me. Then I experienced the pleasant feeling of receiving a scratch behind my ears. Finally, I saw my hand offering me treats from that wonderful yellow bag that had a cartoon cat on the side.

Yes, the voice called into my mind.

"I really must be tired. It's almost as if…" My words trailed off as I filled Purloin's bowl.

Yes, the voice repeated with great satisfaction. As I watched Purloin eat, a part of me wanted to eat some kibble, too, but a quick glance from the cat told me he would not entertain sharing even a crumb. Instead, I stepped back. My head was killing me, like an all-drummer marching band was using it for practice. Still, after all the years I had known him, watching Purloin eat his dinner gave me a feeling of pride.

"Okay, buddy, you enjoy your dinner. I need to talk with Alana and try to apologize. It's never a good idea to go to bed angry, right, Purloin?"

Licking his lips, Purloin glanced at me when I mentioned his name. His expression caused me to laugh. Somehow, he could always convey deep disdain for everything with just a small glance. Images of me talking flipped through my mind, coupled with those same random noises from the earlier version of Alana, and the gruff voice spoke again.

Dumb.

My voice came out in barely a whisper: "What?" At that moment, my phone dinged, and I tore my attention from my cat and focused on the screen. A notification had popped up, stating the file transfer was complete. It took me several minutes to process that information as smaller details came to my attention. For once, there was nothing else running. No apps to close, no playlists engaged. Another absence was my earbuds. With a glance, I realized they were still by my computer, where they had been since this morning. That meant I had never put them in, and they could not be the source of the earlier sounds.

Purloin, having finished his feast, rubbed against my leg in appreciation. A surge of pride tickled my brain, but it wasn't aimed at me. It was more a feeling of knowing someone else was proud of me and would continue to endure my actions despite how dull they found me. Reaching down, I scratched Purloin's ears. "Sorry I missed your mealtime, buddy. That smoke is probably really messing with your nose. Maybe tomorrow I should take you to the vet, and—"

Crinkle skins!

Horror raked across my mind as the visage of a three-headed beast with pale blue crinkling skin loomed over me. Each head called out in a cacophony of sounds: some cooed to draw me in, another was brutally direct, and a third droned submissively.

Before I could react, the creature seized me and began stabbing, poking, and prodding me everywhere. Light flared into my eyes, strange cold rods reached into my ears, and long, sharp nails pierced my side.

No! the gruff voice roared, as the scene repeated in my mind.

Falling to my knees, I let out a sound that I was still not sure was fully human. Breathing became a luxury as I continued to fall and ended up on all fours. Tears poured from my eyes, and my arms wobbled under the strain of holding myself up. Everything was whirling and churning around me. Colors merged and then separated into new combinations.

Kitten! Purloin stepped in front of me, letting out a concerned meow. His rough tongue licked at the tears running down my cheek. At his touch a spark popped between us, and I drews in a long series of ragged breaths.

"What… was… all that?" Rolling onto my back, I lay down, looking up at the ceiling which spun and weaved in my vision. The longer I rested, the more stable it became, and soon I saw a white form looming over me. Purloin's eyes met my own, but they differed from what I remembered. His usual golden amber eyes were now different colors. One was a sunflower yellow, while the other was a sky blue. "Purloin, your eyes…" My heart dropped. *What happened to you? Is that a reaction to those chemicals?* I turned to the ruined experiment on the table. *What was in that vial? I better take Purloin to the vet, see what I did to him.*

The images poured into my mind again, the same beast coming at me, but this time with different tools, fresh pains to bring forth. This time there was a new sensation: separation. I saw myself, or some elongated and goofy-looking version of myself, leaving the room as my perspective stayed caged with the monsters. All around me, I could feel the pain of others and hear their cries of fear for what had or would soon befall them. What stood out the most of my other self was the shirt I was wearing. I had worn it to the vet's office when I took Purloin in for his check-up and went to fill out some paperwork. All in all, I had been out of the room for five minutes, tops. Right after that visit, I spilled some of my pickle brine on my clothes, and Alana convinced me to throw the old shirt away.

No! the voice screeched. Purloin fled, knocking over glasses, scattering papers, and toppling over stacks of books.

Still unsure what to make of what was going on, and happy the pain was subsiding, I rolled onto my side and held out one hand. "Purloin, it's okay, buddy. I'm not hurt. See?" Purloin wasn't listening and continued darting around the room, trying to find a place to hide but only succeeding at knocking over various items and getting himself more worked up. All of his favorite places to hide seemed too small now, and I wondered when Purloin had grown so much.

When I found him, he was barely a handful, and now he was a mini lion. With timing I could never replicate, I snatched up the frantic cat as he passed by me. One hand around Purloin's ribs, I hefted the agitated furball into the air. My reward was a series of scratching and hisses as he continued to flail in my hand. Fed up with his antics and having had more than enough chaos over the last few days, I shouted at him, "No!"

Purloin froze immediately, then turned his head with a shocked slowness. A fresh wave of sensations washed over me: confusion and curiosity, with a hint of offense. It was as if I had never expected to hear those words before tonight. Images of myself came to mind, but this time they were oriented as if I was remembering things through crooked camera angles. Like all the other pictures, they were low to the floor, so I was looking up at myself as I performed various tasks. There was an eagerness to mimic or understand what I was doing, whether it be cooking, cleaning, or playing on my computer. It all seemed so strange, but potentially interesting.

No? The voice asked, testing the word to see if it fit the context.

"Wait." I swallowed, placing Purloin down as I sat up. To my surprise, he didn't run away but sat with his tail wrapped around his feet as he studied me. "Do you understand me, Purloin?" The cat said nothing, as cats were not able to speak in human tongues, but he blinked twice, which was meant to provide confirmation.

I tried something different, something that might get a deeper response. Starting a staring contest, I locked eyes with Purloin and whispered, "Vet."

Purloin's eyes widened, and the images of the three-headed creatures with crinkling blue skin returned to my mind.

No, the voice hissed.

"Food," I offered before he could run off.

Purloin purred, and pictures of the previous meal came to mind.

Food, the voice echoed with satisfaction.

"Alana." Images of my fiancée came to me, mostly of her eating salads, screaming at Purloin when he was on the counter, or pointing a water-sprayer at him. Each image contained a healthy dose of anger yet also had a begrudging respect, like two generals meeting on the field of battle. Purloin continued staring at me, giving off an eager trill. "I've probably gone crazy, but I think you *can* talk, or at least that experiment might have given you the ability to do so."

Visions of me doing a variety of chores came forth, and I could see how odd they must appear from a cat's perspective. Why put chicken in the cold box when it could be eaten? Why not give food to Purloin if you aren't eating it? Why have scratchable things if you won't scratch them? This time, when the voice came to me, it had a dry, sarcastic tone to it. *Same.*

We sat in a staring contest, just watching each other. I had so many questions, and there was so much I wanted to know, but I barely knew where to start. Purloin gave off the impression he was also interested in being able to talk to me but was not impressed by the concept. Now that we had communicated, a growing sense of boredom came from Purloin.

"You're a little cheeky, aren't you?" I laughed, picking up Purloin.

Down, Purloin demanded, sending a series of pictures of him leaping from heights and being set back upon the ground.

Complying, I set Purloin down as gently as possible and he rewarded me with a huff of disappointment and a flicked tail in my face. "This is so crazy."

"Marcus, are you alright?" Alana called out from our bedroom upstairs. "My eyes are burning. I must have used an entire bottle of eye drops. We need to open these windows. There's probably still residue in the air." She came down the stairway with her glasses in one hand, rubbing at her eyes with the other. She leaned back in shock as she looked at me. "Marcus... you're clear!"

With the way the night had been going, I started checking myself out in case I had become invisible or translucent. However, my body was still as it had always been, solid and visible. "No, I'm solid. Nothing clear about me."

Alana gave a short laugh, with just a hint of exasperation. "No, I mean I can see you. Clear as day."

"We've established that. I mean, I'm sitting in the middle of the floor. Not like I was hiding or anything."

"I can see you"— she repeated and tapped at her eyes— "*without* my glasses. Normally I would be as blind as a bat without them. You'd be a blurry blob otherwise." She stopped blinking and looked around the room. "This is so weird. I can make out all kinds of things all over the room, even with most of the lights off. But how? Vision generally doesn't get better after you spill chemicals in your eyes."

Taking a deep breath, I looked from Alana to Purloin. While she marveled at seeing our home in a new light, I replayed things in my mind and tried to figure out how to tell her what I'd discovered without sounding crazy. "I've got some big news, too."

"Is your vision better? I see you're still using your glasses."

"No, something else happened to me." Stopping to steel my nerves, I looked up at her and said in my most serious tone, "I can talk to cats."

She stopped; her expression unchanged. For a moment, I wondered if she had even heard what I said or if her recent change in sight prevented my words from registering. When she spoke, there was a layer of agitation behind her words. She spoke in simple sentences to ensure her meaning was clearly conveyed. "Marcus. Honey. Dear. Of course, you can. Everyone can talk to cats."

My face turned a shade redder as I realized what she thought I was trying to say. "But can *everyone* get a cat to answer them?" Getting to my feet was harder than I thought it would be, but I managed after several near falls. A demonstration would need to be

made, and I wanted to be standing when I did it. "Purloin, food."
Images of meals poured into my mind, and the cat came running
over, meowing with delight.

Food?

"See?" I beamed as I pointed at Purloin. "I just said it and he
came. He even said 'food' back to me and showed me pictures."

She sighed. "Marcus, we do *not* have time for this.
Something could be seriously wrong with my eyes, and you're
making jokes about talking to a cat." She wrapped her arms around
herself. "Purloin recognizes the word 'food' because we use it all the
time before we eat and before we feed him. Of course he
understands it. It just means he learned some pet tricks."

"I know how it sounds, but I can hear him in my head. He's
sending me images of him eating and even repeats the word."

"If he's so smart, ask him what happened to us," she snapped
at me, and I could tell the night was starting to really get to her. To
me, this was all still a dream, but for Alana, it was becoming a
nightmare. Reaching out, I wanted to give her a hug to let her know
it was alright and that things weren't that bad. That it would be okay
in the end. Things were just different, and that didn't have to be a

problem. She pulled away with a muffled grunt of disagreement.

Purloin continued rubbing against my leg; my mention of food had garnered his attention. I got the feeling that seeing Alana and hearing the word 'food' made him think of the meals she prepared, and he thought she was here to provide them. When she turned away from me and toward the kitchen, Purloin took that as confirmation of his belief. Darting past me, he shot between her legs. Like when he tried to hide, Purloin misjudged his size and his back legs smacked into Alana with enough force to move her. With her arms still clenching her shoulders, she slipped and fell onto one foot, toppling forward. The struck leg landed hard, barely missing Purloin's tail, and then she pushed off, performing a backward flip. Even with her arms wrapped around her, she completed the arc and landed with a quiet thump.

My mouth dropped. "How did you... What was..."

Alana pried her hands from her arms with a wince. Four small, quarter-moon-shaped red marks formed on each arm, in the exact places where her fingernails had dug in. "Ow," she cried, checking the severity of the cuts. No blood seemed to come from the injuries. "What happened to my nails?"

My throat went dry. "The experiment. I think it changed us."

"Chemicals don't make people into super athletes. At least not after one dose, and not by an aerosol."

"You obviously have super reflexes and sight. I can talk to Purloin and hear him in my head. We've got superpowers! We're superheroes!" My head swiveled as I looked around the room. "Maybe this was covered in the boring part of the book and I skimmed past it. See if you can find the tablet. The transfer was done, so we should be able to do a quick search about transferring powers or what to do in case of a freak accident."

Alana swept her eyes over the desolation of the dining area, then turned to Marcus with a look that merged confusion and rising anger. "Boring parts? I thought you said you read the entire book."

"I said I looked through it, cover to cover. I didn't *really* read it all, but I studied the diagrams and the recipe." A few seconds of Alana's glare told me I was not helping my case. "Everything was going well until Purloin jumped up."

Up, Purloin echoed, sending me an image of him leaping onto the table. A hint of pleasure filled me. Know that I understood him made Purloin feel proud about teaching me the basics of language.

Pushing through Purloin's projections, I focused on the task at hand. "The transfer of pictures should be done, so we just need to find it and we can look up everything." Under a broken chunk of equipment, I found the tablet. Chemicals oozed out of the casing as I lifted it. Giving it a shake, I tried to wipe it off with a dry cloth before checking the power. After a minute of fiddling with it, I grimaced at the unresponsive machine. "Damn, it's dead. Our only copy of the book and it's dead..." While I debated what to do next, Alana picked up the paper copy.

"Looks like we're going old school. Put the tablet on some paper towels to dry out. Maybe set it in some rice. Besides the mystery goo, nothing in there should have been too dangerous. Until then..." She stopped upon opening the book. "What the hell is this? It's... It's all... blank."

"That happened after I started the file transfer to the tablet. It gave me a prompt to make the electronic copy my key version. After I clicked 'Yes', the book went blank." The face that Alana cast my way made me wilt.

She flipped through the pages. "Paper doesn't just become blank. There must be some trick, but why would an old book be tied to modern software?"

"Maybe it's some variation on invisible ink? We just need to hold the pages up to some flames and it would appear, right?"

"No fire," Alana snapped. "There have been more than enough explosions and run-ins with the authorities for one night."

Taking the book from her, I took a deep sniff, hoping to confirm my hypothesis that it was invisible ink or a lemon juice effect. Instead, all I got was the smoky remains of our earlier experiment. When my finger touched the page, a warm tingling sensation flowed through my hand, and a series of faint lines appeared. The words and images returned, but instead of the faded lettering and ink, it was now all a crisp, clean font. Somehow, the book had become the printed version of high definition.

Alana let out a small gasp and stepped back as if the book might attack her. As far as either of us knew, that could be an actual concern. "That's weird."

Reading had always been a passion of mine. I loved picking up a new book and reading to learn something new. If I'd had more time and had not been through so much today, I might have really gotten into this book. As I flipped through page after page, I started noticing minor details I had missed before. Little marks on the page, etchings that had lovingly been added in a forgotten age. It gave me a nostalgic longing for a time I had never experienced. I could spend hours on each page, learning something new with every line. Where had this insight been before? Was this a side effect of the explosion? The more I looked through the book, the more questions I came up with. I could spend the rest of the night researching this topic, developing theses and writing my own novels on what I gleaned from this book. It was intoxicating how much I could learn. A lifetime could be spent just going through the details in these pages.

Purloin's voice came into my mind. *Dumb.*

My mind reeled at the comment, shifting my perspective up a few levels of consciousness. The allure of the paper and the secrets it held fell away. Instead of experiencing the lines and the wonder they held, I made my way down the page slowly. "This is going to take a while. If only I could just say 'search potential side effects.'"

No sooner had the words left my mouth than the pages flipped frantically forward. The book nearly sprang from my hand,

and I was now focused on the last page. Confused, I pulled away from the book but stopped myself as I saw the exact text I had been asking about. "Was that the paper version of clicking a hotkey?"

Alana circled around behind me, slowly getting closer. "What did you find?"

"Conducting this experiment with an animal can cause Familiar Bonding to occur. This should only be completed under proper observation and with an animal of a temperament that mirrors the magi. For a full list of documented Familiar Bonding side effects, see Appendix F."

"That sounds promising," Alana replied, looking over my shoulder. "But where are you reading that? All I see is the recipe again." I pointed to where I had just read and saw her shake her head. "That's just blank space."

The words *Appendix F* shimmered, and a thought came to me. I touched the term, and again the pages underwent a flurry of motion until I was at Appendix F. One page had a dog-eared corner and nicked my fingertip. "Papercut," I winced before shaking my hand. "Self-turning pages are too cutting edge."

Confusion wormed into my mind, and that same tingling sensation I got when Purloin spoke returned. Something I had said did not register immediately and I could almost hear the mental wheels whirling. As the concepts lined up in my brain, understanding flared into anger. A deep, violent anger. Teeth pierced my ankle as my cat turned on me, assaulting me in his fury. *No!*

"Purloin!" Alana screamed, tearing him off my foot. Long red lines formed where teeth and claw had been dragged away. "What has gotten into you?"

"He hates puns," I answered, twisting my ankle to ensure it still had feeling.

"That makes two of us," she replied, holding up the flailing cat as I hobbled, "but why was he so mad about it? Geez, that cut deep."

"From what I gather, Purloin is learning to translate what I am saying. He thinks all human language—or 'kitten chatter,' as he calls it—is a waste of time. Our inventing language and then making jokes off those concepts was too much."

Alana gave me a blank look and allowed the calmed cat to return to the ground. "If you can't make puns, whatever will you do when you have to make conversation?"

"I can always use my intellect and wit."

"Sure, but that buys you, what, maybe five minutes?"

Yes, Purloin commented, sending me images of pleasing events. I saw myself feeding him and petting him behind his ears, as well as his victories over any stray insects that entered his domain.

"Everyone is a critic," I mumbled, returning to the book. "There is a lot here. Pages and pages of potential side effects." Turning through Appendix F, I saw all the various animals that a person could be bonded to, along with the associated side effects.

What I found most concerning was that none of the entries referred to mental communication; only general intentions and feelings would be transmitted. That would mean whatever I had done was outside the purview of even this odd book. In fact, Appendix F was so kind as to point out a series of warnings like, *Do not attempt familiar bonding during the Witching Hour. Results may vary.* Or my favorite, *One at a time advised.* Whoever had written this book did not know how and where warning labels belonged. If these instructions had fallen into the hands of a moron, things could have gone terribly awry.

Alana picked up a clean piece of cloth and began dabbing at the tooth marks on my ankles. "Pages? You mean you aren't on the blank page at the back of the book?" I pinched an inch of additional pages, but she shrugged. "Is there supposed to be something in your hand?"

"This just keeps getting better and better." I sighed as I settled into the futon. Alana got a wrap for my punctured ankle and instructed me on every part of the cleaning and covering process. When she was satisfied, she started cleaning the wreckage of our kitchen. After an intense situation, she liked to keep busy, and it would be hard to find something more adrenaline-inducing than finding out you had been magically synced up to a cat.

Purloin stared at my covered foot with a confused tilt to his head. "It's a bandage to keep infection out, Purloin. See, there are these tiny things called bacteria—"

Dumb, Purloin cut me off, sending illustrations of all the times my talking had bothered him to prove his point. It took a while.

Not to be deterred by his dismissive comment, I continued speaking while confirming I could still move my foot. Alana had a steadier hand for first aid, but sometimes she made things a *little* too tight. "See, that's why we take you to the vet, to get shots so—"

Crinkle skins!

A wave of fear and hate washed over me, as images of the three headed monster reappeared in my mind. This time, however, I could make out its features with clear distinction. In fact, I recognized their faces and knew their names.

"They aren't monsters, that's the vet and her assistant, Purloin." The words had no effect on his agitation and panic, and my pulse increased until my heart was thudding in my chest. "Purloin…" My teeth chattered. All I wanted to do was run, but my last ounce of will forced me to remain seated. With my final bit of consciousness, I forced out my last words. I'm not sure why my brain picked them, as they would have looked terrible on my tombstone, but before I could stop myself, I shouted, "Bad cat!"

The pressure stopped, and I opened my watery eyes to see Purloin looking at me with hesitation. He let out a concerned meow and walked forward, rolling his head under my hand until I was petting his ears. *Good!* he pleaded, showing me all the times, he proved himself a worthy protector of the home. Purloin purred. A rough tongue licked my fingers when I hesitated for even a moment.

"Okay, buddy." I scratched under his chin. "You are a good cat. We just need to work on your panic attacks."

Best cat, he corrected while replaying his greatest hits. While the images conveyed self-pride, there was also a bit of shame towards me for making Purloin have to provide such a long list.

I best cat. You are kitten, I calm you. Hopping up, Purloin plopped against my leg. Perhaps I was reading too much into the actions of my psychic feline, but the gesture seemed to imply he would stay beside me as proof of loyalty.

"What was *that*?" Alana called from the table. "I step away for thirty seconds and you try to blow up each other's brains, then have a bro moment?"

Purloin rolled on his back, allowing me to scratch his stomach. While I detected a vibe of disdain in response to Alana's remark, he did not seem ready to comment yet.

"The road to recovery is a long path, with many pitfalls and potential brain explosions," I replied, trying to sound cool. I was pretty sure I pulled it off.

"Well, try not to make another mess until we clean up the current one and figure out how to fix all this."

Giving her a nod, I started going through Appendix F. Most of the pages were just descriptions of animals that were deemed acceptable to use in the experiment, including insights into how to best control and corral them for the duration. Even the best-behaved animal would not want to sit right next to an explosion. As the text put it, *ONLY TWO TYPES OF MAGES PERFORM THE EXPERIMENT WITH A LOOSE ANIMAL: THE SKILLED MASTER AND THE FOOL.* I smiled at that line, realizing that everyone who had called me Magus must have recognized my skills.

No matter how many pages I read, another one always followed. I read about finding a companion animal among apes, lizards, wolves, and more kinds of fish than I thought possible, or even advisable, before my eyes burned from weariness. Beside me, Purloin let out a slow and steady breath as he slept. The clinking of glass and plastics and the spraying of chemicals had stopped. A cool breeze came in from the open window, bringing with it comfort and relaxation as I flipped the page to the cat section. The last line I remember reading that night was an additional cautionary comment.

Warning: Using a cat as a familiar can have unforeseen side effects not listed here. Proceed with caution.

"Now you tell me," I whispered before drifting off to sleep.

Chapter 13: Caturday Morning

The next morning, I awoke tucked into my bed as if I had been there all night. Purloin and Alana were nowhere to be seen, and I could no longer smell any of the acrid chemicals from our experiment. "Was it all a dream?"

Still groggy, I lay still and listened to the quiet morning. It was so silent I could hear my heartbeat. As I stayed in my warm bed, another sensation grew in intensity. The soles of my feet tingled, as if I had cut off circulation. A faint, rhythmic pulsing ran up my legs, like an echo of my heart, only quicker and smaller.

Thinking I needed to get out and stretch, I winced as a sharp pain shot up my foot the moment it touched the floor. My ankle was covered, which, while it happened in my dream, could also have been just a foggy memory. Purloin enjoyed random attacks; my arms and shins were covered in tiny slashes. A vicious assault to my ankle would not be unprecedented. Nothing seemed out of the ordinary in our bedroom, but once I reached the bottom of the stairs, I began wondering if I was still dreaming.

Every one of my senses seemed to be under attack. The curtains, normally drawn for privacy, were wide open, sending in the too-bright morning sun. Several items sizzled and popped on the stove, and timers ticked down. If I had not gotten up when I did, the barrage of alarms would have woken me and anything dead within a one-mile radius.

Everything smelled wonderful, and my stomach growled in anticipation. Placing a hand over my stomach, I pressed the sensation down. Not that Alana's cooking was bad, per se. She had made significant progress since she first started practicing; she'd graduated from making ramen and toast to reheating leftovers. Alana considered cooking something she could master, like she had done with laboratory work. "It's just science of a different type," she would tell me. "Follow the recipe and adjust when needed." However, theory and execution were two different things. Often, her meals came in one of two flavors: burned or boiled to paste. Of course, I would say none of these things out loud. After all, she could start the coffeemaker with the best of them.

"Alana." My groggy voice was lost in the cacophony of noises. "What's going on? What are you doing?"

While I could barely hear myself, her head snapped toward me. "Hey there, sleepyhead," Alana called from the kitchen, flipping the contents of a frying pan. "We were wondering if you were going to sleep all day."

Lazy, Purloin agreed, looking up from his breakfast for a moment to send me his opinion of my sleep schedule. Highlights included my posture, my breathing technique, and the depth and length of my naps, including how ugly I was while doing so. As I looked at him, that tingling sensation return, but now it was focused on my forehead. The pulse was stronger now, but not louder.

This was all so much to take in. First, I did not know what had Alana so wound up this early in the morning. Then there was the actual confirmation my cat could talk into my head. Finally, I learned that by cat standards I was ugly. Not the best way to start my day. "What's going on? How did I get in bed last night?"

"I carried you up," she said in a mater-of-fact tone. "I woke up in the middle of the night and you were down here with your head on the table. I tried to wake you, but you were out cold. So I picked you up and got you into bed."

"You... carried me? Alana, didn't you think that was a little strange? Not that you're weak or anything, but I'm not exactly light."

Alana stopped her frantic pacing and looked at me. There was a flicker of realization in her eyes. "That is odd," she muttered. Giving her head a shake, she turned her attention to me. "I've been feeling stronger since I went to bed. I guess I thought it was just being rested and getting a good grip on you. Weird that I didn't consider that until now. I wonder what—"

Outside the house a squirrel was scaling a nearby tree, and she turned her head towards it. Purloin jumped at the window, seeking to kill the prey but only hitting the glass with a dull thump. The squirrel darted further up the tree and out of view.

With the distraction gone, she gave her head another shake and set down a plate of food in front of me that could have fed a family, along with a giant novelty cup filled with coffee. "Come on, eat up. We're going to go for a jog. Can't waste the morning. It's the best time to be awake. Eat, eat, eat!"

"Aren't you going to have anything? I mean, there is no way I can eat all this." Stabbing a sausage the size of two fingers, I gave her a suspicious look. "When did you become a morning person?" Instead of replying, she walked back into the kitchen and started moving dishes into the sink. Bracing myself, I prepared to take a bite. My teeth bit down, and my eyes shot open. "Alana, this is good. Like, it tastes like…"

"Like what?" She leveled her gaze at me.

I chose my words carefully, then shoveled as much scrambled egg and toast into my mouth as I could. My words were a jumble of confused consonants, like a drunk Wookie gargling syrup. When I was able to swallow it all, I gave her an appreciative nod. "So yeah, that's what I was saying. Anyway, what did you do to these eggs? There's something different about them."

"I just seasoned to taste and added seasonings as they smelled right." She moved around the room, cleaning the dishes and putting them away in a blur.

"How much coffee have you had?" I asked, eyeing my drink suspiciously.

"None for me. I woke up full of energy. I grabbed some breakfast and then just felt compelled to do something. It's a beautiful new day. The sun is up and the birds are singing."

Purloin ran back to the window at the mention of flying creatures. My brain pulsed as I remembered what birds were. It was like I was being asked to translate or define a term, but the requestor just took the information straight from my head.

Weakness, the cat commented. I saw how he viewed birds, as tiny morsels that flew because they were too weak to stay on the ground or climb with claws, like a cat would. Instead, birds fluttered around, singing songs, which, Purloin assumed, translated into confessions of their inferiority to cats.

Before I could question the logic of any species bragging about its inferiority, Alana came back to the table, stabbing a few bites of food off my plate. "I was thinking we could go for a jog and enjoy the beautiful weather. Who knows what we might find?" There was a look in her eyes, excitement mixed with a wild abandon. Purloin sent me a sensation of approval, like Alana was finally meeting his expectations for morning energy levels.

Taking a tentative sip of coffee, I began eating again. Even after all my efforts, and Alana dipping in, it was still a mountain of food. "Who are you, and what have you done with my Alana? You hate working out."

She shrugged. "I just feel energetic. I need to do… something. Anything."

"I still have so much food." No matter how much I ate, the

amount never seemed to decrease. "Is there a reason you made so much? Was it going to expire?"

Alana laughed, a haunting, dismissive sound. "Don't be silly. I just figure if we have the food, why not eat it? No need to leave it in the fridge."

"Okay, but doesn't this all seem a little odd? We both know you are not a morning person. Yet you got up and cooked a banquet-sized meal." The side of my face tingled, and I saw Purloin looking at me, or more specifically at my plate of food. He shifted in place, eager to approach and share in my bounty. However, there seemed to be an aura of measured patience, as if there were protocols Purloin was adhering to until I broke my line of sight with the food. "No, buddy."

No?

Purloin tilted his head and sent me images of how he interpreted the word. There was the time I pulled him away from a bag of chips, and he cried out in protest. Next when he was moved off a counter so we could put down the groceries. Finally, I saw Alana taking a piece of plastic the cat had been chewing on. His anger and disappointment at our interference were justifiable reasons to use that word. "No" was a command to show frustration, not an excuse to deny Purloin what he wanted. The very idea of me, as a mere human, having the authority to prevent a cat's demands was unthinkable.

"No," I repeated, and Purloin dropped back to all fours and slinked away. The back of my head ached, and I could feel his eyes upon me as he sent me a series of images about his displeasure. I thought about spraying him with the can of condensed air I kept at my computer and felt a wave of agitation come from Purloin, and his attention must have moved around the room, as the tingling in my head shifted with Purloin's focus.

Scream thing?

Not seeing the can, Purloin seemed confused. He recalled how often I had gotten him off counters or spooked him away from something with a quick spray of air. I had never aimed it at him, as a simple, quick burst was enough to cause him to run.

As I thought about his reaction, I kept eating. "It was just a hypothetical, Purloin. Not real. Just me imagining what I could do."

Imagine? This concept caused Purloin to settle, but he kept his head moving as he watched for the threat. The wheels of his mind turned to process what that word meant and apply it to feline logic.

Threat. He purred, seeing now that I was not warning him that the can was present but that I might use it to prove my dominance. Showing superiority was something Purloin respected, and he settled down for a nap.

"Not quite a threat, just using my imagination to show something I might do."

Dumb. Purloin sighed, illustrating his point by showing me how he thought I looked whenever I spoke. He had no patience for my explanations and found no worth in hearing anything more.

"Oh good. You finished eating." Alana hopped down the stairs, now wearing a neon pink outfit that would have fit in perfectly in a 1980s movie. "Clean up your plate and we can go."

To my shock, she was right. While I was talking to Purloin, I had consumed everything on my plate. But I did not feel bloated or ready to fall into a food coma. Instead, I was satisfied enough for now but also felt like I could eat more if it were offered. Soon, I was full of energy and jumped to my feet. As I washed the dishes, things around me started taking on a more real and grounded feeling. I must have been much hungrier than I thought.

"Are you coming?" Alana called, leaning out the front door.

"No, I'm still waking up. I want to read over that experiment again, see what happened to us. I'm surprised you aren't the one asking these questions. Maybe we should go to the doctor's office to get checked out?"

Alana winced at my words, looking like she had just tasted something foul. "It's not that I don't think it's important or anything. I just feel good right now and want to enjoy it. Besides, what is a doctor going to tell us that the paramedics last night wouldn't have seen?"

"I feel like they could do a lot... Are you sure you aren't feeling at least a little strange? I mean, I'm talking to a cat and you have more energy than you've had in years. Something has changed."

She sighed, stretching to her limits. "But that all sounds so boring, and I don't want to. Let's have fun. It's been a long week, and now we need to take it easy."

Purloin sniffed at the door, planning his escape while we were distracted. While we never forbade him from going into the courtyard, Alana and I wanted to ensure we were around in case he got into a fight with one of the neighborhood cats or dogs. "Purloin," I said, causing him to jump and share his feeling of surprise with me. It seemed he truly believed he, a large white cat, blended into the background of tan walls and thus was invisible to the human eye. "Can you go with her?"

Purloin sat, pretending he had stopped to take a bath and thus could not have possibly caused any trouble. He gave his paw several long licks and started rubbing his ears. Only after three full strokes at his ear did he look at me with his mismatched eyes. *Hunt?* This was followed by a montage of Purloin chasing toys and a laser pointer, plus all those times he *nearly* caught birds just outside the closed window.

"Sure, it's like hunting. Just stay close to Alana. Don't wander off."

Realizing I wouldn't be joining her, Alana started down the steps to our home. "Come on, Purloin." She started at a sprint, and he soon was matching her pace. I watched them until they disappeared in the distance, and that tingling sensation I got from Purloin became smaller and smaller until it felt like a stray hair on my forehead. A minute later, even that tickling vanished. It left me feeling hollow, as if some part of me had been scooped out. I panicked and forced myself to hold the doorframe so I wouldn't run after them. Cold sweat ran down my face until I backed away.

Getting out my tablet, I started researching side effects again. The experiment had just been about making a smoking effect. Just a simple mixture that would be fun to see.

Since I had some time, I examined the tablet. Alana had been right in that it only needed some time to dry out. While it was old and prone to glitches, this old device knew how to take a beating and still turn on the next day. I started comparing the paper copy to the electronic, looking for any differences. It seemed like anything I could do with my tablet was now possible with the physical edition.

Maybe it was my overactive imagination, but I was oddly okay with the idea of magic existing. I can now see that I was accepting it too easily and was taking the situation too lightly. If Alana were in my place, she would have been more studious and skeptical. She would have examined every page, comparing features and abilities for even the most mundane aspects before trying anything difficult. But since it was me, I started trying out random things.

"Cat familiar chapter," I said and watched as the paper pages flipped to the section. The tablet screen flickered and landed on the chapter only a second after. "Paper was a little quicker," I told the device. "What's the matter, not enough battery?"

Next, I placed pinched fingers on each screen and moved them apart. The tablet zoomed in as I thought it would, at the same time the book on the table tripled in size, sending placemats and papers to the floor. Slowly, I pinched the tablet back to the default size and sighed in relief as the paperback returned to its pocket size. "Okay, paper is not as portable."

Finding things and changing the size was cool, but I wanted more. "What's the point of having a magic book if I can't do any magic with it?" Stretching my stiff joints, I looked around the living room. That full feeling wasn't as strong as it had been, but all I had been doing was sitting and reading. How much energy could that have burned?

Flipping the paper pages, I swiped the screen in the opposite direction. They did not sync up. "Well, at least I can research that way. Show me something cool." Both flipped to a section about the importance of proper storage of reagents. That got a dry laugh out of me. "Can a book have a sense of humor?" Pages moved and the screen flickered before returning to the warning about creating a familiar bond with a feline. Despite the humor of the situation, something stood out. *Are they reacting to my words themselves or the meaning?*

Sighing, I began going through the book. What else could I look up? There must be more to magic than just reading and making potions. Alana had superpowers, eyesight like a cat, flexibility, and an abundance of energy. Purloin and I seemed to just be able to talk to each other. Maybe if I read the book again, something would jump out at me. If magic was real, and this experience seemed to prove it, there must be more I could do. "Okay, books, take me to the action spells. Something epic, like shooting lightning or moving things with my mind."

Neither moved. A pop-up reading "user access denied" appeared on the screen of the tablet. *To access more advanced spells, please purchase future editions. Coming soon!*

The book closed itself, and the tablet then powered off. "Some help you are," I told them, not stopping to think about how comfortable I was becoming with quasi-sentient books and electronics or what that could mean.

Start from scratch. My own words floated to the forefront of my mind, and I cracked open the book to the table of contents. My past self was right, and I hated when I quoted myself—especially when that quotation led to doing actual work. However, the haphazard approach had not exactly been a predictable, and repeatable, success.

"Chapter One: Introduction to Chemical Reactions and Stability," I read, hoping that hearing the title said aloud would help hold my attention. That lasted about one paragraph before I yawned and went for a cup of coffee. Returning, I skimmed over the chapter. Overall, it reminded me of my chemistry classes from my school days. Dry and clinical, it discussed the importance of working in a stable environment and following all the rules and warnings. I had to laugh at that point. This book posted all the warnings way after any problems would have occurred.

While the first chapter was less than ten pages, it felt like a novel. The next chapters picked up the pace, and the author's passion for the topic bled through. Chapter two had been about theorems and analytics. Thankfully, it had some diagrams peppered throughout to break up the walls of text, and the author added brief comments under each, stating, *YOU MIGHT ACTUALLY USE THIS ONE DAY, BUT PROBABLY NOT. STILL, YOU BOUGHT THE BOOK. YOU MIGHT AS WELL HAVE THIS.*

Chapter three was about timeliness and solar and lunar cycles. This was where I learned about the Witching Hour and how it could impact and augment chemical reactions.

The fourth chapter was titled "Definitions" and simply said, *SEE APPENDIX D: DEFINITIONS. I WASN'T SUPPOSED TO PUT THIS PART HERE... DON'T TELL ESMERALDA.*

Before I continued, I read the line again. *Esmeralda? I wonder if that's the same person from the website? What was it? Esmeralda's Engines? Equines?* Tapping my lips with my pen I tried to remember the alliterative name for that subsite. "Esmeralda's Equipment." The book reacted to my words by flipping to what had once been an order form, but only the top portion remained. The section I imagined that would have been filled out was missing, probably used decades ago by the previous owner.

Maybe I could get some answers when I was back at work. It

wasn't like the answer was going to come knocking or ring my doorbell, right?

Then, out of the corner of my eye I saw something that might provide some clues. Boxy sat against the wall, long claw marks along his side and a series of tooth marks along the flaps. In the short time he had been with us, Purloin had already claimed Boxy as a new toy, fort, and scratching post all-in-one. But most important of all, Boxy was a shipping box and that meant a return address label would be attached. There might be a phone number I could call for returns and product complaints.

It only took a moment to find the label on the top of the box, but it also only took a second to be disappointed. Purloin, in his eagerness to mark everything with his scent and remove anything that offended him, had chewed and scratched the label into an unreadable state. The spot where you would find a return address was even missing, with incriminating teeth marks along the edge. If I was going to get the address back from Purloin, it would not be in a state I could, or would even want to, read it.

Discouraged that my side quest didn't pan out, I went back to my book. If I couldn't learn from a box, a book would have to do.

Picking up where I left off, chapter five was on coloration, viscosity, and effectiveness. The first line told me this was going to be a doozy. *Finally, we get into the interesting stuff.* In this chapter, the font was italicized so much I almost had to turn the book ninety degrees to read it aloud, "Just as important as getting the right ingredients, you must consider potion coloration type, mixing components, focus, and intent. All of these are necessary to a successful potion's potency. When mixing, remember that a portion of the mixer's energy seeps into the creation of infused items, such as those detailed in this book. Potion effectiveness relies on all things being in balance. Even the words you speak when creating a potion can alter the very nature of the results."

Below this statement was another of the author's notes. *KEEPING A COLOR-CODED CHEMICAL LAB SYSTEM, THE METHODS OF WHICH ARE DESCRIBED IN APPENDIX A, CAN HELP PREVENT EXPLOSIONS AND OTHER PROBLEMS.*

"Finally, someone understands the importance of colors in chemistry," I told the book. "Although you really could work on your warning system. It would be nice to know what could blow me up, before doing an experiment."

The last chapter detailed the experiment I had done, and it remained written in that same blue font. Something I had not noticed last night—in fact, I was positive it wasn't there—was the distinct columns that separated two sets of data. The first was labeled *POTION—SINGLE*, and the second was labeled *TONIC—MULTIPLE*.

"Single? Multiple? Like serving sizes?" I grumbled to myself. "What did I make last night, a tonic or a potion? What's the difference?" No sooner had the words left my mouth than the pages automatically flipped to Appendix D, where I could find a definition of "potion" and "tonic."

Potion: Small dose that can be medicinal, magical, or poisonous.

Poisonous... My heart skipped a beat. Maybe it was my imagination, but I swore my blood felt thicker after reading that word.

"Tonic: Substance with medicinal properties intended to restore or invigorate."

Going back to the test experiment, I started gathering the dishes, vials, and containers I had used last night, checking my measurements against the two columns. Then I went to the section on coloration and viscosity, trying to remember how it looked last night before it all went *poof* in our faces. I wished I had taken notes while I was working and found I had gained a better appreciation for why science journals had so much detail.

Time flew by as I pored through the chapters and references, gathering chemicals and placing them in neat rows while mimicking the layout for a lab shown in Appendix A.

At one point, I got tired, and the book responded by flipping to a section on red potions and the effect they could have on bodies. A light red potion could relieve stiffness in joints and soothe aches. Going to the other extreme, a deep red paste could be smeared over a wound and aid in healing. It could also be eaten, but that might not carry the thicker material to the impacted area.

Before I knew it, I found myself quickly mixing up the ingredients to make a deep red healing paste, which looked more like burgundy paint than any salve I've ever seen. "Looks de-red-ful," I laughed, and an odd feeling came over me. It started at the nape of my neck, then trickled down my arms and into my fingertips. It was like I had pinched a nerve, but instead of a sharp pain it was more like a warm trickle of water running over me. I set the small bowl aside, allowing it all to firm up while I took a moment to study my hands. The sensation vanished as quickly as it had come, and I wasn't panicking at the experience. Instead, I found myself more curious than unnerved.

Rotating my neck in a slow motion, I checked myself for any injury or slight pain. When nothing happened, I made a mental note to watch for that reaction again while I rinsed my stirring spoon in a glass of water. The liquid took on a faded red hue. I wondered if that diluted paste would form a healing tonic or if I was now holding something toxic.

"Not a full dose, just a *pink-me-up*," I said as the liquid in the glass calmed. Again a surge of water energy trickled down my arms. Setting the glass down with a loud thump, I stood upright and held my arms out in front of me. I flexed each finger, examined my arms, and even went the bathroom mirror to check out my neck in case there were any odd marks or discoloration. Once more I was treated to no physical change. *Could I have nerve damage? But then why would it only happen when I was talking? Am I shifting in my seat?*

Returning to my chair, I looked over the glassware and then to my reference materials. Based on my research, red meant restorative, at least on some level. *Could a person become too healthy and then end up sick again? What classified as healing? Could a red tonic cure any poisonous effects my experiment had caused? Maybe I was getting poisoned just by touching these chemicals?*

It was all too much, so I eased everything red, or even slightly in that hue, aside. According to the charts, the next most frequently used potions were those with blue colorations. These were for ailments of the mind and to improve clarity. I made a bowl of thick blue salve, which had the consistency of cake frosting. I fought down my urge to take a bite, despite my stomach's insistence that it would be delicious.

The entire process relaxed me, and I found my mood improving. Just as the mixture thickened, I felt compelled to comment on it. It was like a burp forcing its way out of me, pressure that would not be denied its escape. "Food for thought, or thought for food?" This time when the warm sensation hit, I wasn't unnerved but I was getting annoyed. Looking deep into the cool blue frosting-like material, I saw something sparkle.

"What is wrong with me?" I asked aloud, and without Alana

and Purloin around, I was forced to answer my own questions. Holding up the blue-covered spoon, I took another glass of water and stirred. An idea formed in my head, and I wanted to try out a little hypothesis.

When the material had washed away from my spoon, I held up the glass and watched the swirling water until it nearly became still. I racked my brain for the right words and just as I found them the water steadied itself. "Will this work? I'll find out in blue course." Sure enough, that feeling of warm trickling energy flowed down my arms. It felt small, like more was trying to flow but was blocked by something at the source. I looked into the blueish water as the sensation reached my finger-tips and for just an instant saw a flicker of something spark inside the liquid.

My hands were shaking as I set the glass down, causing small bits of charged drink to spill onto the table. Then I threw my head back and screamed in sheer and utter delight. "I did it!"

I wasn't sure how I knew, but I was certain that I had just performed a feat of magic. Of course, there was also the possibility that I had just suffered nerve damage from last night's experiment and all I did was replicate the sensation.

Somehow there was a correlation between my wordplay, or the puns I used, and the sensation in my arms. I just knew there had to be a change to the liquid and paste. With a few more tests I was sure I could continually replicate the results. There were several more colors and combinations, but I decided to only try one more for the day: yellow. According to the book, these were focused on energy. Unlike in the other recipes, where there were multiple types and hues, this one only listed the mixture for a light-hued variation.

A small box listed the only warning in the appendix:

Any yellow substance more potent than those listed here should not be attempted as a tonic, potion, or paste. See infusions and thoomological concoctions for more on working with yellow.

"What in the world is a thoomological concoction?" I muttered. The pages of the book flipped forward per my command. "No. NO! Not when I am in the middle of something else, you stupid book." The pages slowed, drooping over until they stopped completely. A twinge of guilt hit my heart. Had I just offended a book? "Sorry, book," I offered. "You're not stupid, I just got over excited." I held a finger to one corner of the page. "Still friends?" A little fold of paper curled up to bop my fingertip. I smiled a little, until the realization that I was talking to a book, and that it was replying, sunk in. The idea made me uncomfortable, and I decided it was best to leave this mystery for another day. Right now I needed to put the giddy energy from my discovery to good use. "Let's go back to yellow potions, okay?"

A short time later, I was mixing up a yellow concoction. I watched the materials fizz and bubble together. When it all settled, it appeared I had made a watered-down glass of lemonade. I spun the glass on the table to examine it from each side and ensure everything had dissolved. Stopping the spin, I let the contents slow. Just before it went still, I spoke. "Watt did I just make?" As I had hoped, the warm flow occurred and a crackle of energy rippled over the surface. I let out a deep sigh. While I was excited, I also did not know what it all meant. I was also tired, like I had run several miles and was only now stopping for a breather. My head slumped forward and my eyelids fought to stay open.

I wanted to write all of this down, and move on to the next phase of the process. All that was left was to test out what I had made. What would I try first? Healing salve? Medicinal potion?

Maybe the blue mind frosting or the glass of mental clarity? There was also the lemony looking energy drink. Any of them would be a great test, but the real question was how would I test them?

Sure, I could pour some onto a plant, but it wouldn't tell me what was happening to it. It might be even worse if I could see a physical reaction. The last thing we needed was a meat-eating plant or for it to have some other mutation. A talking cat was already going to be a handful. I didn't need the ficus giving me lip, or eating me.

The next option would be human or animal testing. That concept was not even worth considering. Last night was enough human experimentation, and I would never ask anyone else to drink a strange substance I made in my homemade lab. So how was I going to see if my work paid off? Had I really made magic chemicals, or was I just playing with pigments?

All that thinking was thirsty work. My hand instinctively reached out, and I took a sip of my drink. Two things hit me at that point. First, I did not have a drink at the table. I had purposely kept anything not related to the experiment as far away as possible to avoid a repeat of last night's events. The second thing that hit me was a bolt of crackling energy on my lips.

All I recalled was a loud *pop* and my lips stinging. A wave of force threw me from the table and into the living room. I hit the futon and rolled over it, crashed onto a table, and rolled to a stop against the wall. To my delight, and also dismay, a weak whine escaped my lips. On the plus side, I was alive and had survived two magical accidents brought on by my negligence in about a twelve-hour span. On the negative side, I had been in two explosions.

Images of myself lying on the overturned furniture and groaning in pain popped into my head.

Dumb.

Chapter 14: Do Not Try This at Home

"Marcus!" Alana screamed, her footfalls sounding far away. Her face filled my vision, and my head wobbled as I focused on her. I never realized quite how deep brown her eyes were. "Are you okay? Speak to me."

"Don't drink the lemonade," I wheezed.

Alana worked on freeing me from the rubble while Purloin sniffed the air in disgust. "What were you doing? Why are your lips so puffy?"

She helped me onto the futon, and I fought to keep my head from spinning. "Just making some potions. Took a drink of the wrong one. It had a kick to it." I wasn't sure if I was trying to be funny at that moment or if my brain just couldn't find any other way to get my point across. Maybe it was a side effect of my potion making. "That yellow stuff is basically liquid lightning, and it's in its diluted form. We should really put down a towel or something..."

As I battled for coherency, Alana raced around the room. She threw a towel on the table, soaking up the spilled liquid, and plopped the half-empty glass into the sink. "I can't believe you, Marcus. Experimenting with potions, again, after what happened last time.

No, you know what? I *can* believe you would do that. What I can't believe is you would do it again– and when you're alone."

She picked up more broken pieces of furniture, cleaning up the mess I had made. The way she tossed broken boards aside, it was like everything was made of cardboard. I tried to sit up, but everything hurt, especially my back.

"Geez, Marcus, we need to get you to the hospital. We should have gone already, even if the paramedics cleared us. I knew the equipment in that ambulance looked old. I bet it was out of calibration too." Her eyes were rimmed with worry. She shifted between moving toward me and going for her purse and car keys.

"I'm just a little sore," I lied, trying to divert her away from my battered state and maybe calm her down before panic could set in. "Besides, I think I figured out my skills. I can make magic potions by telling them puns. Sure my nerves feel pinched afterwards, and it runs up both arms for a bit, but it's not really that bad overall."

The look on Alana's face showed me she was not taking my discovery with as much excitement as I had hoped. "I'll get my keys," she said.

"Did you enjoy your run?" I yelled, getting her to stop before she made it too far. "Find whatever it was you thought you were looking for?"

She stared at me for a long moment, breathing through her nose as she studied me. "I know what you're trying to do, Marcus. You can't distract me with side topics, not this time. We are all going to get checked out again. Purloin started getting queasy as we ran. It almost looked like he was getting smaller. I hit runner's wall and could not catch my breath. Coming home, I started feeling better, but we need to go in for tests and take Purloin to the vet."

Vet! Purloin hissed, backing away from us. *No! No go.* He arched his back and pulled a hiss of utter hatred from the depths of his soul. His shoulders arched as he backed away toward the stairs. *No!* He spat into my mind, bringing up images of the three-headed monster. When his hind paws touched the stairs, he whirled and swung one paw forward. Tiny razor-sharp nails dug into the hardwood with a loud *thunk*. One nail caught and Purloin tried to pull it free. However, it was lodged in too deep and remained fixed in place. Panicking, he thrashed and fought, but failed to remove his paw. Wood popped and chipped from the stair. Then, with a final mighty pull, his claw cracked the plank.

Before our eyes, Purloin grew until he was the size of a lion. He still looked the same, just enlarged to a great cat's proportions. Rage and fury crackled across his blue and yellow eyes. The broken piece of wood clattered to the floor in front of him. He growled, turning on us.

No vet!

The thought repeatedly echoed in my mind.

"Purloin!" I shouted, holding out a hand to catch his attention. My heartbeat raced. I had seen lions and tigers before, but usually it was on TV or safely behind bars at the zoo. This was something else. Seeing my little buddy grown into a primal, prehistoric beast was terrifying. I tried to stay calm, to speak in a calm manner, but my jaw trembled. Every part of me wanted to run, but my body was in no shape to stand, let alone put any amount of safe distance between me and this creature. Purloin loomed over me, an angry predator finding defenseless prey. "It's okay, buddy. No vet. Stay. Home."

Out of the corner of my eye, I saw Alana glancing at me. "Purloin," she said in the same tone she used when trying to find him. "Good kitty." She raised her hand, mimicking my motion, but I gave a slight headshake to stop her.

"Don't move. He might hurt you." As much as I wanted to get out of there, I also did not want Purloin's attention to shift from me. Even in his rage, a part of Purloin's mind registered some part of me as worthy of holding off the killing bite. The feeling was a mix of kinship and ownership. By clamping down on my exposed neck, he'd be breaking something he enjoyed. I can't say that gave me much confidence, but right then, I was glad to have any sort of buffer.

Alana nodded, becoming still, and maintained eye contact with Purloin. When she spoke, it was barely above a whisper. "What should we do? Is he saying anything?"

"I'm getting a repeating message. He's tired. Plus, I can see what he thinks the vet is. To him, it's a place we take him to get hurt. He's feeling threatened. Now he is ready to defend himself. He doesn't understand things like doctors or medicine."

"Marcus, this isn't natural," Alana whispered. At that moment, I think the idea of magic being real started registering in her mind.

Purloin's anger pressed down on my mind, his fury pouncing on the quivering fear of my thoughts. Blood trickled from my nose as the pressure grew. My body ached and Purloin must have felt some residual effect of that pain, as he let out another hiss. I needed to stop him before he hurt himself or one of us. If he could send images and emotion to me, maybe it could be used the other way. First step, calm him down. Dull the pain that throbbed along our mental link. *What I wouldn't do for an aspirin right now...*

Alana was trying to move, to position herself to help me if Purloin lost the last of his restraint. She slid ever so slightly toward the end of the futon. As she did, light from the window glittered on the glassware.

The table! Of course!

"Alana," I said, speaking as low and slow as I could. She made no move to look at me. "Alana," I said again, still slow but putting a bit of force behind my words. This time she cast me a glance. "Do you see the glass?"

"Yeah," she muttered in a whisper. "What about it?"

"Can you bring it to me?"

"What is it?" She started toward the table, but when Purloin's eyes moved to her, she froze. His nose flared as he considered what to do about the standing female.

"It's a healing potion," I answered. "I just made it. If you can give it to me, I'll drink it. That should soothe some of my pain and might calm down Purloin so I can talk to him."

Alana was shaking. "Marcus, I keep telling you Purloin can't be talked to, can't be trained, and you've already blown yourself up with one potion. You're crazy if you think I'll let you drink that stuff."

"Alana," I whispered and Purloin snarled over me. "What other choice do we have?"

She stood stone still for several seconds. From my vantage point, it felt like I was waiting hours for her to decide. Then she acted. Darting to the table in the blink of an eye, Purloin soared over the futon as if gravity were merely a suggestion. He plopped down between Alana and me, arching his back and letting out a furious screech.

She backpedaled as Purloin's large leg came down in a white blur where she had just been. Liquid splatter onto the floor and I prayed it was from a glass and not from Alana. Purloin let out a horrified screech as one of his nails caught in the floorboards. It seemed he was not yet comfortable with how much force he could use and how weak the wood was against his massive claws. Wood splintered and cracked as he fought to free his trapped nail.

Alana appeared beside me, propping up my head and holding the glass to my lips. As the liquid sloshed toward me, I glimpsed it just before it entered my mouth. "Not the blue—"

Blue liquid poured down my throat, and I experienced the mother of all brain freezes. Every part of my sinuses tensed, and I learned that parts of my head I didn't know I had could hurt. I shoved Alana away, breaking off the flow. With my next breath, the sensation went from squeezing pain to an icy wintergreen freshness. It was like my head was stored in a cooler filled with mint.

On the other side of the futon, Purloin let out a strange *n' yat* sound. I dully wondered if he had ever had brain freeze before. It was not what I had wanted, but the momentum of his anger had been broken. I couldn't move my body, not without pain and stiffness, but I could think and let my mind wander. When the sensation of Purloin's mind touching against mine registered, I started thinking about our home, about sleeping in my bed. I imagined how warm the light was that came in the front window and how soft the fur was behind Purloin's ears. *Safe. Home. No vet.*

No vet? The lion-sized Purloin asked, plodding over to the end of the futon. The anger that had been pushing against me ebbed. His mind still shook with a deep fear, but the fury wasn't burning in his mind. Instead, Purloin was mentally circling me, looking for a trick or some weakness I was hoping to exploit against him. I swallowed hard and raised one hand. Needles of pain shot up and down my arm, but I focused on maintaining the link and staying calm, on separating the body from the mind. Purloin licked his lips, showing off his dagger-sized teeth as he took a cautious step toward my upturned hand.

It's funny the things you think about when you're looking down the muzzle of a massive predator. Everyone talks about how their life flashes before their eyes, about how they see loved ones and long-lost friends, or about dreams they would never see come to fruition. For me, one image came to mind, and I could not make myself think of anything else. It was the first time I held Purloin, when he had fallen from under my car after his under-carriage adventure and stalked up to me, demanding attention. I remembered how small but fierce he had seemed.

Small? He stopped, his long white fangs mere inches from my face. Another series of images flipped across my mind. Purloin as a kitten sleeping on my lap, the grand climb to his tower looking out the window and into the courtyard, his ability to squeeze under anything to escape my reaching hands. Lion Purloin looked at himself.

Big!

Taking a chance, I stroked the fur on his neck. I hoped that if he did panic, I could at least push his jaws away from me, but even with Purloin distracted, there was no give in his frame. "Small," I echoed aloud. "Little Purloin, my kitten." Large eyes shifted to me. Moving my hand behind his ear, I scratched that spot Purloin just couldn't reach on his own. He closed his eyes, and pleasure trickled into my mind.

Big, he whispered through the connection.

"No, small," I repeated, continuing to scratch. Alana looked to me, and I nodded toward his tail. She ran her nails along the base of his tail, where it met the spine, and scratched.

"Small kitty," she echoed. While I could feel Purloin's

annoyance at Alana's intrusion, the pleasure of getting petted overcame that agitation. We continued to pet him as I encouraged him to think about being small.

Blue and green mist wafted off him in small tendrils, matching the smoke from the experiment. Slowly, Purloin shrank until he had reached his original size. Alana stopped her massage, and I reduced my speed until Purloin opened his eyes and met mine.

Small, Purloin repeated. He looked at us, shifting his gaze between Alana and me. There was a tinge, just the smallest start of a speck, of respect in that view. Maybe, just maybe, there was even a hint of embarrassment behind it, although I doubted Purloin would ever admit that to anyone.

With the crisis averted, Alana let out a long sigh. "Okay. This is getting nuts. If we are going to be living with magic or whatever has happened to us, we need to be smarter. We can't be freaking out." She looked at Purloin, but the tremor in her voice gave her own feelings away. "That will require safe and controlled testing. Use the proper tools to test this and conduct research."

That was Alana. She might panic, but she was quick to make a plan. Purloin curled up on my chest, trying to settle in for a nap.

"Before we do anything else," I groaned, "hand me the red drink."

Chapter 15: Testing

The red potion worked as promised, healing my aching and battered body. I was in no shape to run a marathon—not that I ever could, mind you—but I wasn't in miserable amounts of pain either. However, I soon discovered that drinking blue and red mixtures within a short time of each other had a... gaseous side effect. I wish it had been only belching. At least that would have made the ride to the hospital more pleasant.

Looking back, I'm not sure if it was good fortune or a cruel twist of fate, but our hospital visit was quick and uneventful. Although it still took until the middle of the afternoon.

Alana told them about our smoke inhalation, referencing the police report from the previous night and how we had experienced a shock.

My doctor examined my head, and I told her about my loss of consciousness and the nerve pains. She ran tests and gave me some fluids, but everything came back negative. Medically speaking, I was normal. More tests would be run in a few weeks, but for now, she could find nothing wrong with me. The same results came in for Alana. With clean bills of health, we went home. The doctors advised I take a week off work to rest up, since I was a mess of bruises and sores. I took that as a win, while Alana thought I was just looking for an excuse to be lazy.

Purloin greeted us before leaping onto his tower for his routine nap. The morning's events must have really worn him out because he did not even lift his head when I gave him his lunch.

Alana looked over the paperwork from the hospital, displeased at our clean bills of health. "This makes absolutely no sense. There must be some change, something measurable. How long did they tell you before the blood work comes back?"

"A couple days, maybe a week?"

"That long? I could run these tests in a few hours if I had my lab…" With a groan, she slapped the papers down only to pick them back up and review the contents once again. "You know what? No. No." She grabbed her keys and gave me a determined look. "I still have my lab, even if it might only be for a little while longer."

"Alana," I protested. "It's been a long enough day, why don't we just calm down for now and relax?"

"Relax?" She shouted, a manic energy in her eyes. "How can I relax, Marcus? We've been exposed to strange chemicals, started having crazy behavioral and physiological changes, and might even be in legal trouble for having that vial."

"True," I stammered, "but wouldn't going into work to use the lab equipment be even more illegal?" Picking up the red book, I tapped the cover for emphasis. "I'm sure the answers are all in here. Sure it might be written by a crazy person, or probably by a whole asylum, but the experiment did something. There must be an answer in here."

She looked at me, then at the book before shaking her head. For a moment I thought she might hiss at it. "I don't trust that book. Nothing good has happened since it showed up. But I trust the scientific method."

"What about me? Do you trust me?" I tried to give her a reassuring smile.

Alana shook her head. "I do, Marcus. I really do, but not with this. We need a lab and proper equipment if we are going to figure this out. Not just fanciful theories."

I swallowed my disappointment and gave a weak laugh. "Don't you mean hypothesizes?"

She laughed and gave me a quick kiss on the cheek. "I love

you, Marcus. Let me do this for us, while you and Purloin stay here. I think it's time to toss all this junk, and move on from all this craziness. No more conducting experiments, alright?"

Giving Alana a slight bob of my head, I looked over my scattered supplies. "I'll get started cleaning and put some stuff back in the storage room. Heck, this might be just the motivation I need to finally make a workstation in the storage room for all my other projects." She smiled, gave my arm a quick squeeze and then was out the door.

As the car pulled out of our parking lot, I started gathering up the mess I had made. Occasionally, my eyes would rest on a note or drawing I was scribbling. Thoughts began bubbling to the surface as I tried to put the house in order. *Is it even possible to go back to the way things were before last night?*

The experiment altered my brain. I could now talk to a Purloin. I suppose I could always hide that as just being really in tune with my pet. Purloin huffed in disgust at the notion that I outranked him.

Alana's alterations were physical in nature. She was more agile, able to do a backflip from a standing position. Her eyesight was nearly perfect, she could see even the slightest movement or tiniest flaw on something. Plus, her other senses had become enhanced, which helped her not burn the eggs and season food to an excellent level of taste. Hearing her upstairs, I began wondering what else about her may have changed. Would she sleep all day like Purloin? How catlike had Alana become?

A chilling thought bubbled up in my mind. Could she eventually become a cat? Could I? How much more could we change? Was all of this magic or some kind of old science that mankind had forgotten? A part of me still wanted it to be magic, even after everything we have been through so far.

We still didn't know what that chemical was or understand the full extent of what it would do to us. My stomach gurgled. What other effects could all of the other potions I drank have on me? The tests might not show us being affected, but maybe that was simply because we were changing in ways that no current tests could identify.

Dumb, Purloin groggily put into my head, then drifted back to sleep, thoughts of mouse and insect hunts playing in a loop at the back of my mind.

With too many questions left unanswered, I would not give up just because things got complicated. There was work to do today. I pointed to the stairs. "Come, faithful Purloin! To the lab!"

Chapter 16: Ringing My Bell

It turns out Purloin was not faithful, or at least not willing to follow me. As I went up the stairs to the storage room, he merely rolled over and continued his nap. He didn't even take the time to insult me for trying to make him move; instead, he mumbled something into my head. Alana would call it being grumpy, but I found it kind of cute that cats could mutter.

Alana made me promise not to conduct any more experiments, and I planned on keeping my word. However, the loophole in that logic was I could still do things related to the topic. Case in point: I was going to renovate the spare bedroom into a magical lab.

Well, renovate might be too strong a word. What I was really going to do was move some shelves around and bring everything related to our project upstairs. It was a little smaller than our bedroom, but instead of bedroom furniture, it was filled with old folding tables, shelves of various heights, and all the odds and ends I had collected over the years. The room was also a haven for new species of dust bunnies.

Throwing open the window, I took a deep breath of clean late afternoon air. I really should have set up everything in here from the start.

For the rest of the day, I dusted off counter space, moved boxes to form makeshift workspaces, stubbed my toe multiple times on oversized pickling jars, and organized my collection of random things into something resembling storage.

"A place for everything." I picked up a box of miscellaneous items and dropped it behind another row of boxes. "And everything out of sight."

The small desk I had been using to store boxes now looked more like a real science lab. Vials, beakers, glassware, and chemicals were all lined up in neat rows, with plenty of workspace still available. In the box of cookbooks, I found an old spice rack that made a great makeshift storage for powders and small containers. By the time I hung it mostly straight on the wall, I had made three separate holes in the wall. Still, it now offered me somewhere to house containers that Purloin might decide to knock out off the table. Even if I explained why he shouldn't do it, he was still a cat.

No more reaching over other components to find what I

needed. I even cleared enough space to take notes and have either my book or the tablet on the surface. All of the remaining room's clutter was now in sorted piles.

All that was left was to bring up the potions and salves I had made yesterday and wash up. As I trotted down the stairs, a prickling sensation raced across the front of my brain. It was coupled with a series of images of me running under beds, tables, and futons. *Hunter*. The images that followed were of eyes looking out of bushes, large dogs from the neighborhood, and Purloin's distorted image of a veterinarian.

Multiple bangs came from the front door, which nearly flew off its hinges with each blow. *Is that another delivery? Maybe it's someone about that delivery yesterday? Good, then I can get some answers from them. I'm not in any mood to be pushed around.*

Grabbing the vial of strange liquid I headed to the door with determination. If this person was going to try giving me an earful about accepting a package meant for a company, or that I should have corrected them on delivering here instead of having them to take it to Wonderland Pharmaceuticals, then they were going to answer my questions. As I opened the door, I had my game face on.

I held up the strange vial, so that the first thing this person would see is my grim expression and the empty container.

The figure on the other side of the door was not the delivery man from yesterday.

Solomon stood like a monolith in front of my door, tall, unmoving, and with an aura of ages old menace. Seeing him in sunlight felt wrong and I understood why Purloin thought a predatory beast was outside. He must have heard Solomon approaching and ran. I wish I could have done the same.

"Hey, Solomon," I said in my best cheery voice, extending my free hand and lowering the vial as quickly as I could. "I didn't know you made house calls? Is Mr. Payne with you? Was that order—"

Solomon's giant hand covered mine, and he pressed something into it. When he pulled away, I could see he had given me a vial wrapped in a sticky note. The same vial and note I had left on my desk. He inhaled sharply, waiting for me to speak. From his uniform's front pocket, he pulled out Vincent Payne's platinum credit card just enough to send a message.

Based on my limited understanding of how moving walls speak, I figured he must have been telling me, "I went to get the card and found these things. Answers now, or I break you."

As I looked into his large vacant eyes, my friendly smile faded. The hair on the back of my neck stood on end, and Purloin sent images of going under the bed, jumping into boxes, or running behind shelves.

Hide.

Fighting my unease, I forced myself to at least appear jovial. Maybe it was my imagination, but I could have sworn the wind had died down and my neighborhood had suddenly gone silent.

"I know this looks bad, but it's actually nothing. Kind of a funny story, really. I have some questions about that stuff I ordered for Mr. Payne. See, one vial fell out last night." I held up the empty vial and saw the big man's eyes open wider. That was the first hint of emotion I had ever seen on his face before. A small part of me hoped that meant this could solved easily and that Solomon would go away. I did not like the thought of him knowing where I lived, and especially did not like the idea of him being at my home. "I was going to bring it in first thing on Monday. I guess I could have gone in with Alana, since she's at work right now, but one thing led to another, and the experiment went—"

My words died in my throat as Solomon reached out and grabbed me by the neck with one thick hand. He lifted me off my feet as if I was made of Styrofoam and squeezed. "Got it all wrong," I gasped. "I stole nothing. Didn't—"

Purloin meowed from under the futon, fear flooding my brain. Not that I needed help being afraid right now. "Purloin," I whimpered, but he remained safely hidden. There was no rational way he would justify attacking something as large as Solomon.

The big man scanned my home, looking for whoever I had been talking to in case he had to silence any other witnesses. Not seeing anyone, he turned his focus on me. His head tilted, as if he was expecting something or thought I could reply while being strangled.

If I could just break his hold, I might find something to defend myself with or at least cause enough of a ruckus to get someone's attention. Some part of me laughed. *Ruckus. Alana's right. I really should update my vocabulary.* A light went on in my brain, but thankfully it wasn't the one at the end of life's tunnel.

Vocab… words… puns.

"Wait," I wheezed, trying to pull open Solomon's vise-like grip. Sentences were impossible. All I could do was spit out a syllable at a time. As my vision blurred, the faint whine of my words seeped out. "Feline… potion… sleep."

Solomon continued to glower, his eyes smoldering with contempt as he looked me over. But he eased his grip enough for me to suck in a little breath. Air had never tasted so sweet, and my lungs filled with a shuddering inhale. Even with my windpipe no longer being actively compacted, getting out every word was still a force of will. I had to choose them all carefully. The next sentence I uttered could very well end my life.

"Knocked. Me. Out. …. Made. Me. Cat-a-tonic."

Power erupted through me, starting from the nape of my neck and down through my arms and legs. It was as if for the first time in my life I was truly awake and alert. Solomon's grip broke, as the smell of burning flesh wafted from his massive palms. He staggered back, and I wasn't sure if he was more confused by what I said or what had happened. The surge of power surprised me as well, but that answer would have to wait. My words hadn't been for Solomon.

I could have talked all day and not bothered him. Purloin however, hated puns.

The tingling of panic and fear at the base of my skull flickered, like a radio struggling to maintain a signal. From behind me there was a loud thud of more furniture toppling over, and I prayed it wasn't another of Alana's ceramic figurines. Then a white comet soared at my back. Falling to the ground, I left Solomon at the center of the missile's trajectory. Purloin, now having grown to a lion's size once again, collided with the colossal man. The two flew off the porch with Solomon taking the full brunt of the assault and landing hard on the concrete.

Purloin sprang off him at the last moment, landing a few feet away. Solomon let out a grunt, which sounded more surprised than hurt. Still, I was happy to hear something had fazed the homicidal giant. Purloin had already turned and was moving on his opponent.

Fight, he growled into my mind. I wasn't sure if Purloin realized I had tricked him into getting mad, but right now, I was happy to have the time to breathe and stand up. My legs felt like they had been replaced with broken lead weights.

Purloin pounced, shoving his claws into Solomon's shoulders. The large man growled back, an unnatural rattling sound, and grabbed the cat's legs, trying to free himself from the pin. Purloin flexed his claws, digging the dagger-like nails deeper into his enemy. A low steady growl rumbled through the massive cat, just before he lunged at Solomon's exposed throat. Solomon grasped Purloin's jaws, stopping the glistening fangs just before they could close on his flesh.

As the two titanic creatures battled, I got my legs under me and rose to my feet. Still dizzy, I looked around for anything to help Purloin fight off Solomon. Nothing stood out. No knives, heavy pans, or tools were in sight. I plodded forward a few steps, nearly falling over as I coughed for breath until I collapsed on the counter, looking into the sink. Maybe there was something I could use, something we just hadn't cleaned and put away. But all that was in the sink was a nearly empty glass and a wet dish towel.

A wet towel covered in explosive energy juice! Grabbing the cloth, I twisted a thick stream of liquid into the empty glass. Behind me, Purloin howled in pain. Solomon had twisted the cat's legs and threw him aside with a deep grunt. Purloin was righting himself, his legs twitching at the fresh injury as he tried to adapt. The big man stepped forward and swung his massive fist at my cat's head, and there was a wet crunch before Purloin fell over. Shards of pain assaulted my brain, my eyes burned as tears ran down my cheeks, and my heart wrenched until I thought it might rip free from my chest. I was in misery that my brain could hardly comprehend, but my heart immediately could identify. Purloin was dying, and I was feeling every moment as if it had happened to me.

Reaching the door, I let out a scream as I came running out the door at full speed brandishing the wrung towel in one hand and a glass of yellowy water in the other. "You've done enough damage, Solomon. You're going to pay, and you better have cash." He turned to look at me, long red streaks coming from his shoulders where Purloin's claws had been. Despite his injuries, he looked more annoyed by this battle than concerned. My left arm swung back, letting the towel crack like a whip. He looked at my weapon and brought up a large arm to easily counter my pending attack.

Instead of bringing the towel forward, I let it drop and tossed the liquid contents of my glass forward. Just as the liquid hit his face, power surged through my body once again. "Never mind. You can charge it."

The liquid splashed over Solomon, and, for once in the last few days, there was an explosion that was *not* centered on me. Starting as a pop, like when a lightbulb blew, it expanded into a rush of pure force. The wave of energy knocked me flat onto my back and hurtled Solomon backwards into, and then through, his car. Metal was crushed, glass broke, and tires let out an ear-piercing screech as the car was pushed across the concrete.

"Yeah," my voice cracked. "That's your pun-ishment for messing with Marcus Kyle, Magus Pun.H.D." Admittedly, that wasn't the best trash talking I could have done, but overall, I'd say it wasn't too bad for my first victory speech.

Rolling to my feet, I looked at Purloin. Blood poured around his eyes, and his tongue hung out, looking more purple than it should. I knelt before him, tears welling in my eyes. "You stupid cat, why?"

Protect my kitten. Purloin sent images into my mind, showing me all the times, he had tried to instruct me in the art of being a cat. These were all from before the time when I could understand him, back when he had thought I was just a fellow feline who didn't know the rules. The thought that *he* could be the dumb one made him chuckle. His gigantic eyes flickered towards where Solomon had been moments ago. *You. Cat now.* A feeling of peace seeped into my thoughts. His mission felt completed, and now it was time for rest. A nice long rest.

"Stay here, buddy. Don't move. I'll get help. I'll get..."

Medicine? He sent me images of him being forced to take pills and the struggles I faced when forcing them down his throat.

I ran back into the house, trying to think of what I could do. His skull looked cracked. My cat was broken, and I didn't have the skills to fix him. All I could do was break things, blow them up, blow myself up. My only success seemed to have been mixing potions.

Potions! The paste!

Tossing aside various vials and bottles, I scoured the table until I found a small bowl filled with red paste.

"This has to work," I told myself as I flew out the door. The paste was thick and crusting over. *I should have put a cover on it. This might be dried out.* My heart broke as I applied it to the bloody wound marring Purloin's white fur. He growled and hissed as I administered the red goop, sending me several messages showing how much he hated this and, by extension, me. It was hard to see where I was applying the deep red paste as it was the same hue as the blood on his fur. The tears pouring out of my eyes also blurred my vision. "Gah," I hissed, wiping at my eyes as I tried to focus on the injured area. Some of my medical goo got in my eyes, making it even harder to see as it mixed with my hot tears to give my vision a crimson hue. No words came to mind as I tried to think up a pun to add to the potency of the paste, but that surge of power from earlier had faded and now I was drained. Something had opened inside me in my moment of panic, but now there was no gas left in my tank.

I don't know how long I knelt there, rubbing paste into Purloin's wounds. Besides being partially blinded, the pain I was experiencing second hand from our mental link provided a constant sense of urgency to my actions. After what felt like hours, but realistically couldn't have been more than seconds, I no longer felt the sharp lines of cracked bone along my fingers. *That means the medicine is working, right? The wound is closed.*

Purloin's coarse tongue lapped across my hand, like cold wet sandpaper across my skin. With my blurry and tinted vision, I turned to him, and forced myself to smile. "You're okay now. Good as new, buddy." My body shook. I blinked to clear my eyes. "Up!" With one last wipe at my eyes, I could finally focus on his face. "Treats?" I offered, hoping food might motivate him to get up.

Purloin blinked twice at me, then closed his eyes. Relief washed over my mind. The pain from the injury was replaced with a mild euphoria as Purloin let out a long, tired sigh. His breathing slowed, and our link became calm. Then it went quiet. His chest no longer rose or fell.

Standing up, I clasped my hands over my eyes, unable to hold back my tears. I had done everything right. I stopped the monster and healed my companion. So why, *why*, was he not moving?

Something sharp dug into my ankle, needle-like daggers burrowing into my uninjured foot.

Imagination.

Purloin, who had shrunk himself back to his original size, was now wrapped around one of my feet, his teeth digging into my ankle. Dragging him off me and leaving long red lines on my leg, I gave him a big hug. My brain flipped between anger and joy, and I embraced both by squeezing the protesting cat. Affection was never Purloin's strong suit.

"That's not how imagination works." I tried to laugh, but it came out as a muffled hack. I reached out and scratched behind Purloin's ears. He gave my hand a polite lick in reply. Eventually, he flailed free of my hand and trotted back into the house.

Food.

As he retreated, I turned my attention to the wrecked car. Or at least, I looked where the car Solomon had rocketed into should have been. Because in place of a decimated hunk of metal and broken glass, with the body of a giant on top of it, there was nothing.

Nada. Zippo. Zilch.

Where had Solomon and the car gone? Why weren't the neighbors running out with all the noise? Police sirens should be getting louder already.

Instead, I was standing outside of my townhouse looking at a perfectly normal parking lot. My hands trembled. Had I imagined the fight with Solomon? The aching in my throat told me I had been choked.

But could that be an effect of the potions I've been drinking?

Was all this nerve damage or a mental break-down?

I'm not sure how long I stood outside looking into the night, trying to find the hulking giant that had attacked me and Purloin, and to locate the mangled remains of his car, but night had fully fallen when I finally went inside. I knew what happened was real, and that I wasn't crazy.

One thing became certain in my mind as I shut the door behind me. Alana was wrong. We couldn't put all of this behind us. Something big was going on. Something bigger than her, than me, and even Solomon himself. Alana might be on the right track with her research, but I didn't need to just sit back and let her do everything.

I had been looking at things from the wrong perspective, the little red book hadn't been a fun read on feline tricks. It was serious reading.

"Time for me to turn some pages."

Epilogue

"I'm going to stop you there," the woman behind the lights announced. "We need to listen to someone else for a bit."

"But I haven't even gotten to the most relevant part that got us here," Marcus offered.

"Yes, and that's why we are changing speakers," another voice chimed in, this one still muffled by the modulator but more eager and excited. "All you've told us is your introduction to magic story. Everyone knows that magic is the first language, and puns are language at its peak."

Marcus mouth dropped. "What? How do you know—?"

"Never mind that now, magus. We'd like to speak to the cat if you don't mind."

Marcus coughed into his hand. "I just told you, he can talk but only to me. I could translate if you would like."

"That won't be necessary," the first of the voices stated. "We will take our chances. Please move the cat's chair to the microphone and take a seat by Ms. Kym."

Purloin meowed his concern as his chair was moved in front of the microphone. A quiet chirp escaped his mouth as he peered at the male human. "I know, buddy," Marcus said, trying to comfort the cat. "They just want you to tell your story." Giving the cat a nod, he added, "Yes, I am aware. I know you don't want to."

The white cat shifted on his pillow before looking at the microphone with concern.

Two steps away, Marcus stopped and sighed. "Yes, you can have a treat after this. Just hurry it up before they get mad."

Purloin let out a sad exhale, concerned that Marcus might not keep his promise.

"Okay, kitty," the voice called. "Please begin."

Shifting his shoulders, Purloin meowed. Marcus grasped his head and staggered to one knee.

"Marcus!" Alana left her chair, racing to her fiancé.

"Ms. Kym! Please return to your seat," the voice commanded. "We need you all to stay put while we sort—"

"My fiancé is in pain," she hissed, helping Marcus back to his feet. "We don't exactly have a lot of time. You know what happened already, and you know what's out there. I told you already. We need proper medical attention, not to be playing twenty questions with shadows and flashlights."

"It's alright, Alana." Marcus winced, staggering back to one foot. "It was just a lot to take in at once. Help me to a chair, and I'll be okay."

Purloin meowed, concern in his voice.

"Yes, buddy. I'm alright enough to get your treat later. Don't worry."

Letting out a pleased sniff, Purloin watched his humans take their seats and looked back at the microphone. It was time for his tale to begin.

Betrayal...

Acknowledgements

1. <u>Gaby Michaelis: Beta-Reader and Editor:</u>

   An avid lover of stories who has helped both published and unpublished authors make the best out of their novels. You can contact her at:

   https://wanderlostborough.wordpress.com

2. <u>Bodie Dykstra: Editor</u>

   A Canadian editor who specializes in self-publishing. You can read more on his website:

   https://sww.bdediting.com.

3. <u>Gerard Conte: Cover Artist:</u>

   Gerard is a freelance cartoonist that lives in his hometown of Brooklyn, NY. After graduating from SVA, his work has appeared in digital projects and print publications for The Smithsonian Channel, Zenescope, and Comicbook.com. When he isn't at the drawing board you can probably find Gerard working on an old Jeep.

   https://www.gerardconte.com

Made in the USA
Columbia, SC
26 January 2023

10277966R00124